THE LOVE WARRIOR

Also by Alan Lacey and available from NEL:

A LAND WITHOUT MERCY

The Love Warrior

ALAN LACEY

NEW ENGLISH LIBRARY
TIMES MIRROR

ACKNOWLEDGEMENTS

I am grateful for the kind assistance of the following people: The Rev D. Rees for advice on the storyline and for correcting my manuscript; Mr Michael Harrison for inspiration out of the past; Mick Brooks for country vibes; and E. C. and G. C. for memories of realism.

A New English Library Original Publication

*

FIRST NEL PAPERBACK EDITION MAY 1975

*

NEL Books are published by
New English Library Limited from Barnard's Inn, Holborn, London, E.C.1.
Made and printed in Great Britain by Hunt Barnard Printing Ltd., Aylesbury, Bucks.

45002271 4

FOR PETE,
A FELLOW WANDERER IN THE COSMOS

Prologue

Kristabel pushed the thread through the eye of the needle, and then focused her attention on Calisto. She has the eyes of her father, though he only had one of them when I knew him. Her skin has Ylain's softness, Cheiron used to say . . .

'What did my father do before he came to Acima, to the Dale?'

She has her mother's colour in her hair, like a hayfield, but its texture is like that of Cheiron's, thick and ruffled . . . 'Many things, Calisto, so many, many things. He told me often of the place where he came from, and the fine people of the great city he once knew, and whom he scorned. He told me of his adventures before he reached this place . . .'

'Tell them to me. Tell me all that my father told you, Kristabel, I will have to know. I must continue where he finished . . .'

The middle-aged woman pushed the needle into the material and looked at the fair-haired girl, a mere sixteen of what Cheiron had called 'Standard Years'. Kristabel pushed her greying, wispy brown hair behind her ears and began to tell Calisto what Cheiron had told her a long time ago. As she recited the stories to Calisto, Kristabel found herself wondering: What else was there to this story? What were the details? What words did Cheiron exchange with the people he spoke of? Who knows? Cheiron used to say that most of those with whom he spoke were dead. Poor Cheiron. Who will lament your passing now? Who is to know what you suffered, and why . . . ?

It began, it began on New Earth. New Earth . . . a long time ago . . .'

PART ONE: THE CHOSEN PLANET

For this is the way of humankind
The way shall be subtle
Paved with human greed, lust and pride
And, upon occasion,
There shall be love
Leading ultimately to a greater love.

. . . *Echoes of Destiny.*

Cheiron Androcles

The top of the canyon framed the cloudless sky and narrowed the rays of the sun from the yellow rocks down on to the knot of riders in the bottom of the canyon. The riders were swathed in white so that only their eyes, hands and feet were exposed to the shimmering heat. The horses, too, were white. But there was gold and silver about these men also. Long sabres hung from their waists and some nursed electron torches in their laps as they waited.

Cheiron Androcles looked nervously around the canyon. To his satisfaction, his men were invisible behind the rocks. His riders were fidgeting behind him. He had a sick sensation all over his body which sat immersed in the folds of the sun-blankets. His senses were alert, in anticipation of what was to come. His eyes sweated and stung from the heat together with the nervous ache of his body. When will we hear them? he wondered, what will we see? They may take us so fast that we shall see nothing. Perhaps they will destroy the canyon entirely . . . But then these aren't ordinary soldiers; these men take delight in their slaughter. The Peacemakers enjoy most to slay by the sword. They will try to split our ranks with torches first. They will succeed unless my men in the rocks can fire first . . . and the Peacemakers are footmen; in these conditions their transporters would be useless. But we must strike hardest before they can call up an aerial attack . . .

Xenophon came to the Senator's side. His pale green eyes

flashed over the canyon and then he turned to Cheiron. 'They are trying to make us nervous with the waiting, I suppose,' he observed.

Cheiron turned to Xenophon. 'I don't think that the tribesmen realise what sort of enemy we face. Perhaps success has swamped their minds so that they are no longer able to face a greater opposition than simple men with empty bellies.'

'There you underestimate the men who follow you, my Lord. It is trained into them to enter into each encounter as a fresh encounter, as though the enemy were completely unknown to them. They will never grow too conceited in battle because they want to go on living, but that doesn't mean that they are incapable of dying for a cause.'

Cheiron sighed and felt his breath moisten the veil of the sun-blanket. 'I have never felt quite this way about a battle before, Xenophon. We have never faced the Magnate's own forces before now. I fear for the survival of what I have achieved in these lands. If the Magnate is victorious, it will probably mean a reversion to the Old Ways.'

'That is the reason we stand here today. The Magnate knows that we have achieved what is right, but that was his task and not ours. He will make his own rules and start all over again. He's afraid of being undermined on New Earth. This is the hub of the Second Empire, and if the hub decays then the wheel will collapse.'

'We think alike, the Magnate and I,' Cheiron said with a hint of humour in his tone. He turned his gaze from Xenophon and looked patiently along the jagged canyon. From around the bend, about five hundred metres in front, a stream of blue water trickled from a spring to flow along until it became sluggish and brown and flowed into a cave after turning a semi-circle.

I've seen him in battle many times, Xenophon pondered, watching the big man from the corner of his eye, But never have I seen him so distant. Does some destiny call him? The way he seems to smile to himself under his blanket, the way his hands clutch the reins of his horse show it. His thoughts seem to be vague if I am to judge from his eyes and the way he sits bolt upright. His thoughts are rarely vague. He is too exacting. He even pretends to look blank to draw men out blindly to give him the truth or the lies that he wants to hear from them. But today he is genuinely far-off in his mood. Xenophon looked around at the Senator again. I must try to draw him into caring again. 'Eurysaces has positioned his men farther down the canyon as you ordered, my Lord, but he expresses concern at their defenceless position. The slopes tend to be more gentle further along and the shale doesn't afford much manoeuvrability in the spaces. The position seems to be altogether too open for a front-line defensive system.'

'That's the point, Xenophon. Eurysaces' men are not meant to be front line defences. They are an offensive body. We have to strike first. I agree about the shale, though. Have the men moved up higher, but not too high because I don't think it wise to have them huddled in the rocks when the time comes to advance or fall back. What's your opinion?' Have I satisfied him? He senses my mood. I must not permit my feelings to become infectious, it might cost us the battle and what we have striven for for so long. Why am I in this frame of mind? I don't seem to be able to control my strategy, I can't coordinate my forces properly. So much depends upon this battle . . . that's it. I'm tiring of the responsibility. Not even Xenophon could think of me . . . and yet I am getting tired . . .

'I agree that they ought to move up higher. If the Peacemakers try to scale the slope, our men can retreat to the rocks and handle them with ease . . . but what about attacks from the air? Our men'd be completely without cover.'

'We'll hit them hard before the aerial stuff comes in and then we can start thinking about getting under cover. Now, go and see to those men and hurry back. I want you with me when they come. I don't want to lose you of all people today, too much depends on both of us.' Good. Now I'm thinking better. Ha! Xenophon was trying to snap me out of my mood. Was I wrong in taking Xenophon as a friend? Xenophon has too much knowledge of humans. He can translate their emotions into what he pleases . . . He can mould their thoughts to the way his motives swing. Could anyone swing Xenophon? The Magnate? What would Xenophon do if confronted by the power of the Empire condensed into that one man? Are there others like our Xenophon?

Xenophon rode off down the canyon and swiftly away round the bend in a flurry of dust. Cheiron watched the dust settle. He became aware of his horsemen behind him. The collected tribesmen of the nation of the Aoidni stood against the Peacemakers of the Second Empire of New Earth. They faced them on their own ground. And yet they knew that the ground was not unfamiliar to either of them. This was New Earth . . . the hub of the Empire. Suddenly, Cheiron was entrapped in the web of a spider, almost ready-wrapped in the streaming grey fibres . . . suspended in the larder. Is this why I tire of the responsibility? Do I yearn for absolute freedom? There can be no absolute freedom on New Earth. New Earth is the political gem of the galaxy. New Earth is a bloated ball of papers and politicians. There seems no room for people any more. No room for nations such as the Aoidni. New Earth is a centre of administration . . . full stop. I have tried to change that in my own way. I have succeeded with this nation up until now, and yet there has been so little time for *me* to feel free from administration and responsibility.

Xenophon returned some time after and joined the horsemen at Cheiron's side once more. 'I've seen to the matter of the men on the slopes. Now what, my Lord?'

Cheiron looked into his lieutenant's eyes. 'We have only to wait, Xenophon,' and then he turned back to his vigil of the canyon.

Machaerus the Peacemaker

The valley twisted and contorted until the valley was a canyon, and even the spidery trees and coarse grasses ceased to flourish among the rock.

On the banks of the little river, Machaerus' council tent had been pitched. The white tent seemed to glow in the noonday sun. In the relative cool of the interior, Machaerus was sprawled awkwardly across his chair in an attempt to be comfortable. He wore no armour, just the light undergarments which he also found less than comfortable. He was unused to such conditions, having been stationed in the regions surrounding the capital city for five years, mostly sitting at a desk in his extremely comfortable contour chair. He missed that chair. He knew that he was becoming soft in his middle age, but cared little about that since no one was about to make that observation aloud.

Native attendants stood around the circular walls of the tent paying attention only to the whims of Machaerus and nothing else. Opposite the general sat a tall, lean man with a thin moustache and an olive complexion. He was dressed in a white, one-piece garment with a large, rounded collar which gave shade to his neck and the back of his head. Short black hair was pressed flat on to his rounded skull and plunged around his ears. His hands, fumbling on the arms of the chair, were encrusted with various gems but despite his rich appearance he seemed unperturbed by the lowliness of the field equipment of the Peacemakers.

For long moments, Machaerus simply looked at his guest and fidgeted in his chair. Then he said: 'So, my dear Duke Dolophious, you come to me at the very last possible moment in the hope of saving the life of a miserable rebel for your own purposes.'

'The Magnate has told me that he wishes to leave the decision in your capable hands, Machaerus. The Magnate is a busy man and I think that he regards this matter as rather trifling.'

'The Magnate regards this entire affair with care, but without interest. The situation is difficult. Should I make the wrong decision, my Lord, the security of the empire could be put at stake. The Magnate would be less than pleased with me.'

He is infatuated with his power, this Peacemaker. How can such a rising upset the Empire? Perhaps I should humour him? 'I can assure you, General, that where I am sending this senator he can cause very little harm to the Magnate or to you. I am assured by my people that his presence there will be rewarded with rather a rich gift for the empire . . . rich beyond your dreams, General. That is why I want this rebel, because he is the only man that I can think of who would be able to pull off these delicate negotiations.'

The general showed mild interest. 'Er – these "negotiations", would they concern your own estates in the empire?'

'Of course they concern my *estates*, but not actually those within the boundaries of the empire. They concern the expansion of the Empire.'

'That would seem to suit the Magnate's policy. What do you mean by "expansion"? How far do you wish to expand your territory? I seem to remember that your duchy lies very close to the Confederacy of Planets' territory.'

'That would seem to be the point, General. I have discovered an entirely new trading route by which our ships can reach the Great Belt of Trading Worlds without going through the Confederacy or around it for that matter. If we can achieve this, we can end our trading links with the Confederacy of Planets altogether. To achieve this aim requires a minor expansion of the Empire. We would have to take just one planet and that is all.'

'That's dangerous territory to move in. The Confederacy might regard such an action as being aggressive towards them. Besides, what has Cheiron Androcles to do with all this?'

The Duke shifted in his seat and crossed his legs. 'As you know, General Machaerus, the Great Belt lies just outside the far extremity of the Confederacy of Planets. The Great Belt is the centre of trade in the galaxy. From the belt come all the basic needs for planetary colonisation units and also various luxury items which show a nice profit – '

'Get to the point, I don't want a geography lesson.'

'It is essential that you fully understand the situation. I shall be as brief as possible. So, you understand the importance of the Great Belt of Planets. Essentially, they are controlled by the Confederacy of Planets because of its proximity to the Belt. The area is screened by deflectors so that ships from our empire can't penetrate the Great Belt by travelling through Hyper-space. We have to send our vessels around the Confederacy and then approach the Great Belt in ordinary space. This represents a time loss of about twenty Standard Light Years. That's why we rarely send ships to the Great Belt. But it so happens that just outside the confines of my duchy there is a space-warp. This is a very particular space warp, though. It is in the vicinity of a solar system which has been categorised as "Phi-Omega Three". But we have discovered something rather extraordinary about this system. It has ten satellites, only one of which is habitable and it just so happens that the habitable planet has a revolution of its sun once in every three hundred Standard Years. But for a certain time during each revolution, this planet passes through the space-warp and if our calculations are correct it emerges somewhere in the middle of the Great Belt. It stays there for just over a century before passing through the warp again and emerging back in its original position for the next two hundred years.' He paused to make sure that Machaerus understood, then continued: 'The planet was first discovered one hundred and fifty-two years ago but the nature of its orbit has only just been realised.'

'Has anyone ever been there?'

'Only the Tellers. And this is where Cheiron Androcles comes in. The planet is inhabited by a minority of the humanoid intelligent species. Most of the planet is covered by radioactive material. We only know about the people there from the Tellers, and they are vague about it anyway. It appears they have a definite cultural system but their society is primitive. We know little else, only scant details. The atmosphere of the planet is impervious to scanners and so on, so we can only rely on what the Tellers say, and they don't say much. The Tellers seem to have a lot to do on the planet; some religious significance I suppose. Anyway, you follow what I'm getting at?'

'I think so. You want to colonise this world and sit and wait until it goes through to the Great Belt again and we have a century or more of free trade in the Great Belt. You were saying something about Cheiron Androcles.'

'Ah yes. As I said, there are primitive life forms on the planet. These have to be brought into the Empire – but not in the standard way. A conquering force of Legionaries could cause suspicion in the Confederacy to say the least, and this has to be kept secret. Should the Confederacy discover our plans then they will quite simply screen off the planet. No, we have to be subtle. We have to win the inhabitants over to us, get them to accept us. There is one man that I know who can handle them – Cheiron Androcles. I am sure that Androcles can do this. By the time the planet makes its transition it could be safely in the power of the Empire of New Earth.'

'In the same way that the lands of the Aoidni have been won over to Cheiron Androcles and are now independent of the planet on which they are situated . . . ?'

'Something like that, yes.'

'I can't see why so much rests on this one man, my Lord.'

'He has proven himself. One slip and the natives of the planet would avoid contact with the Empire and then we'd have to resort to the Legions. I can trust Cheiron Androcles to pull this off.' Machaerus regarded the Duke cautiously. He heaved himself out of his chair and walked round the tent. The Duke's eyes followed him. He looked down at the groundsheet thoughtfully. 'I wanted Cheiron Androcles for myself to destroy. I have a personal score to settle with him.'

Oh no! That's all I need! This general could get in my way now. He doesn't see through my motives, and yet now there is another danger from a rather more uncontrollable quarter: the man's emotions. Will he risk everything to settle this score of his?

'You see,' Machaerus began, returning to his seat. 'Cheiron Androcles hates me and I hate him. He calls me a war-monger and I call him a hypocrite. This has been going on now for years. We had a number of quite famous debates in New Incarnation over the policy of the empire and we both gained and lost in them. Then he went rebel. I almost had him busted at the time, then he busted himself.'

'I see. I can offer you no compensation for your loss, I'm afraid.' That should appeal to his sense of 'loyalty to duty' etcetera . . .

'Well, we all have to make sacrifices. I'll take Cheiron Androcles alive for you, my Lord, and then we can discuss this more fully.'

Pompous idiot! I'd like to see you killed in the battle today whilst flaunting your so-called power! 'That seems reasonable, General. I'll watch the battle with interest.'

'It will not be very interesting, my Lord, unless, like my men, you are a sadist.'

Duke Dolophious grinned at the general.

Duke Dolophious

As soon as he left the tent, the Duke began to perspire. The dust hung in the baked air. The men moved about sluggishly, carrying their weapons and armour around with them. Some sat playing games while the pilots reclined in the flight-decks of their stratospheres. There were four 'spheres in a neat row at the rear of the encampment. They each towered forty metres over the camp, gleaming bright red in the sunlight. The flight deck was situated just above the repeller-projectors which formed a wide, continuous band around the diameter of the 'spheres.

The Duke walked across the camp to the first stratosphere and stood beneath the hulking monster. It was balanced on four flimsy legs and mainly supported by the repeller-panels on a small collar in the centre of the 'sphere's underside. Occasionally, the repeller rays caused electrical flashes in the air and they hummed and crackled. The Duke felt the hairs on his face tugging and his hair fluttering though the day was still. He found a small box-like control panel on one of the legs and pressed his signet ring into a circular dent. The panel lit up and chattered, and then a hatch slid open at the top of the leg. An elongated tube slid down the leg and the Duke moved aside. It settled on the ground, the Duke stepped into the tube, the repeller panels hummed, and the tube retracted up into the hatchway which closed beneath it.

The Duke found his way to the flight deck and greeted the three-man crew. He then positioned himself in the passenger couch and waited for the order to move from General Machaerus.

Eventually, the Peacemakers were ordered to fall in and shortly afterwards they began to march. The pitch of the repeller rays grew louder and the stratosphere began to jostle as the pilot raised the legs and the rays balanced the machine alone. Then the 'sphere began to ascend gradually and hung over the army at the rear.

'They're sending the soldiers in first?' the Duke asked the pilot.

'Yes. They don't want us to deprive them of their little game.'

The army pressed forwards with its weapons at the ready. Bright armour gleamed in the sun and banners unfurled as the men talked in excited voices.

They turned the next bend in the canyon and the stratospheres hung back. There was the loud and terrible sound of electron fire and the occasional clash of arms.

'Take us up higher so that I can see what's happening,' the Duke ordered. The pilot nodded and the stratosphere climbed above the walls of the canyon. The Duke left his seat and looked out of the viewer at the battle raging in the canyon below. There was dust, smoke and noise everywhere. It looked for a moment as though the Peacemakers had pushed right into the heart of the canyon, then the horsemen of the Aoidni charged full tilt into the shining ranks and there were screams as the scene became engulfed in red smeared on silver . . .

After an hour, the order came from the General for the stratospheres to move into battle. By this time, the Peacemakers were halved in number and displayed little of their former confidence. The Duke smiled inwardly to himself, and thought: So, Cheiron Androcles proves himself a match for the Imperial Peacemakers. I wonder what the dear General is thinking now. I only hope that he is able to take my prize alive . . .

The stratosphere swept downwards into the canyon again. Electron beams bounced from the hull several times before the 'sphere's x-ray laser cannon put a swift end to the offenders hiding in the rocks. Two more short blasts cut deep into the horsemen and sparked off a hasty retreat. The other 'spheres moved in on either side and the ground hissed as the lasers struck in a flurry of flame and intense light.

The Duke craned his neck, trying to catch a glimpse of Cheiron Androcles somewhere below but it was difficult to distinguish anything definite in the tumult of the battle. Then, quite suddenly, there was the sound of an explosion that caused them all to clap their hands over their ears. They caught a glimpse of the hull of another 'sphere crossing their viewer and then their craft was jostled aside and the ground below jumped and shook. There was another explosion and one of the 'spheres swept along the bottom of the canyon until it bounced and struck up against the canyon wall. The next moment the picture on the viewer was swept aside as several savage-looking rocks were hurled at the viewing panels and the picture erupted in a mass of red sparks and fragments of machinery. The floor toppled and then flames danced throughout the flight deck. The Duke felt his head crash against the ceiling and then his body drop to the floor with a hard smash. Then . . . stillness. The craft lay crippled as sparks flew around the flight deck, providing the only illumination now that the daylight no longer flowed in from the viewers.

The three crew members lay slumped over their controls. The Duke was surprised to find himself still conscious after the crash. He pulled himself up from the floor and found that the 'sphere had landed so that the flight deck was at a steep downward angle.

The Duke climbed the steep incline to the hatchway of the flight deck. He opened the hatch and was confronted by a twilight scene of destruction. Blackened cables draped limply over smashed and hissing pieces of equipment. Buckled plates drooped awkwardly around. It seemed an impossible task to find his way through the tangled maze. Eventually, however, he managed to struggle through and feel his way to the elevator hatch. After shifting parts of the shattered tube aside, the Duke opened the hatch and looked down at the smoking ground. Suddenly the sounds of the battle reached his ears again. It was a long way down from the hatch, far enough to break a limb in a jump. The Duke turned back into the 'sphere and looked around. He crawled back a short distance and then kicked the landing gear several times until the insect-like leg was persuaded to collapse limply out of the hatch. The Duke huddled down as tight as he could to avoid being whipped out of the hatch by the flailing leg, and then it dropped and the 'sphere creaked as the leg dangled from the hatch.

The Duke clambered down the blackened protuberance and then ran along the ground to get a view of what was happening in the battle.

All four stratospheres had come down. One had exploded on contact with the ground. They must've collided, the Duke guessed. He looked around. The canyon was littered with bodies and there was the noise of fighting somewhere far-off. Then there was the sound of running, followed by hoofbeats. The Duke dived to the ground behind a dead Peacemaker and watched as a group of soldiers ran across the canyon pursued by a group of horsemen with whirling sabres. The soldiers followed their unmistakable general, Machaerus, while the leader of the horsemen was also quite unmistakable in his stature and utter ruthlessness.

The Duke rolled over the body he was lying behind and snatched up the Peacemaker's electron torch. The riders cut into the soldiers who collapsed under the slashing blades. The General fell, grovelling, in the dust. He pointed his electron torch as Cheiron Androcles appeared over him. The Senator urged his horse backwards, realising that he had tugged at the reins too late . . . The Duke aimed and pressed the firing stud. The General let the torch fall as another torch screamed characteristically as it unleashed its beam. Machaerus clutched at his devastated chest and fell backwards as the life fled from his body.

The Duke sighed and stood up. He looked at Cheiron Androcles calmly. The Senator hauled his mount around and galloped over to the Duke.

'Sorry that was a bit messy,' the Duke said. 'But there wasn't much time to adjust the angle of the beam. It seems that you owe me a favour, Cheiron Androcles.'

The Senator dropped the veil from his face. Xenophon and the other men came to his side. 'I owe no man a favour,' Cheiron said, 'least of all an imperialist.'

'You do me an injustice, sir,' the Duke argued, dropping the torch. 'Perhaps you are jealous that it was I who put an end to Machaerus and not yourself.'

'I do not glory in death. Who are you?'

The Duke bowed. 'Duke Dolophious Thesprotus of the Grand Duchy of Phistars, at your service.'

'You know that I am Senator Cheiron Androcles. This is my friend and *Hemit Thea Epop Y Us*.'

Xenophon nodded.

'Honoured, sir,' the Duke said.

'Why did you save the life of my Lord, Sire?' Xenophon enquired.

'I have a proposition to put to Senator Androcles. I remind you, you do me an injustice when you call me "imperialist".'

'Traitor then?' Xenophon asked.

'No more nor less a traitor than Cheiron Androcles.' He looked into the square set face of the Senator probingly. He turned back to Xenophon who also dropped his veil to reveal a pale, oval face. '*Hemit Thea* . . . I sense something of the Teller in you, Xenophon.'

'My mother was a Teller, my father a prince of the Aoidni.'

'I, too, have Tellers' blood flowing in my veins, though only through ancestry. As you seem to have won the day, may we retire to a more comfortable place to discuss what I have to say?'

Cheiron thought for a moment. Who is this Duke Dolophious? I know him only by his title, but what is the man? He says he has Tellers' blood . . . I must have time to speak with Xenophon about him. 'There is a village a few kilometers distant where we can use a council hut.' Cheiron turned to his men; 'Hippothous, give your horse to the Duke. Try and round up the mounts which have strayed during the battle. Find Eurysaces and tell him we travel to Hypsipylon.'

The man nodded and dimounted. The Duke walked to the horse and Hippothous handed him the reins. Cheiron and Xenophon secured their veils and the group of riders started off along the canyon towards Aoidni territory.

Acima

Cheiron and Xenophon left Duke Dolophious seated in the council hut at Hypsipylon whilst they went outside to discuss the man. The evening was gathering over the village as the army of the Aoidni returned from the battle and flocked into the parched streets on their horses, carrying as much loot as each could manage. They were greeted by the excited children, the councillors and the whores and the fires were lit and a festival was begun which would last well into the following day.

Cheiron and Xenophon stood in the street as their soldiers and the villagers rushed and laughed and sang and danced in the firelight.

'What do you make of our guest, Xenophon?' Cheiron asked his friend.

'He has Tellers' blood as he says, but not much. I sense a great feeling of *fate* and *destiny* about the man, but it isn't just the man alone . . . '

' . . . This "proposition" of his perhaps?'

'Perhaps, my Lord. To get a clear idea of this I would have to read the stars.'

'Just for now, tell me about the man.'

'He is noble-born but he isn't a terran. I feel the omniverse in his character, something that says he prefers the open and infinite space . . . perhaps something of the Teller in him there, the wandering instinct. His mind is dominated by the physical, however. He has a political and technical mind rather than a conscious mind suited to the Teller within his soul. He may also be devious, a spinner of plots and intrigues . . . but he has a streak of blatant honesty.'

'Certainly a strange trait for a noble-born. I will talk to him about his proposition.'

Xenophon put on a mask of deep purpose: 'Have a care, my Lord. I have said that I sense great destiny behind this man . . . your decision over this might have effects more far-reaching than you can imagine.'

Cheiron nodded and then turned back to the closed door of the hut. He opened the door and entered, followed by Xenophon. They both removed their sun-blankets and flung them into the corner of the hut and then walked to the collection of chairs and benches gathered around the empty fireplace. The Duke relaxed in a chair laden with animal furs and he smiled as the two men approached him.

Cheiron and Xenophon dropped into two of the chairs and looked at the Duke for a while. Cheiron was tall and lean with his face seemingly constructed of square blocks whilst his nose was rounded and as incongruous as his lips. His black hair hung thick and straight around his head and brushed the dark skin of his neck. He wore light red undergarments and a large pendant, the insignia of his leadership hung around his neck and rested on his chest. Xenophon, also, wore a pendant which represented the twelve signs of the Lords of the Zodiac and which was the insignia of the Tellers, but it included the words *Hemit Thea Epop Y Us*, and the pendant might have been a description of the mysteries of Xenophon's pale green eyes. His eyes gleamed as he looked at the Duke, their colour clashing with the flame-red hair that caressed his oval face and matched his pursed lips which contained a hint of cruelty.

The Duke became nervous in the silence. 'Well, gentlemen, shall we begin our discussion?'

'You were going to make a proposal, my Lord,' said Cheiron, blankly.

'You understand that the utmost secrecy must be maintained over this matter?' the Duke asked. He looked into the faces for a reply.

Xenophon nodded thoughtfully: *A great feeling of fate and destiny. Yes.*

'I have your word?' the Duke wanted to know.

'For what it is worth,' Cheiron answered.

Duke Dolophious thought about that for a few moments and then declared: 'So be it,' and went on to describe the background to his proposal as he had done earlier in the day to General Machaerus. When he had finished he said: 'I told Machaerus this afternoon about this. As with the Magnate himself, I put him under the impression that in this endeavour I was looking after the interests of the Empire, I don't have to tell you that my main interest is my own profit and, more so, my prestige. I shall be rather an old man by the time the planet emerges into the Great Belt; but there will be many business men clamouring for rights to goods and transport and so on before then and the Magnate might well be tempted into handing over a handsome reward if I can secure a foothold for the Empire on the planet.'

'You mean if I can secure a foothold for you, my Lord,' Cheiron corrected him.

'Of course, Senator.'

'Perhaps you'd like to tell me what I'd get out of all this.'

This should prove interesting, Xenophon thought.

'I have,' Duke Dolophius began, 'exceptional bargaining powers granted by the Magnate himself. I can offer you all of the following things: a free pardon for yourself and your colleagues; legal, semi-independent rule for the lands of the Aoidni together with a seat of representation in the Senate and the Imperial High Court and other such government offices; government development grants of up to 800,000,000 Imperials for these lands, together with the guaranteed protection of the New Earth security forces while still maintaining a policy of strict military non-interference.'

'That sounds very generous,' Cheiron said. There was a hint of sardonic humour in his voice. 'But there is one thing I'd like to know, and that is: what happens to me when my work on your planet is finished?'

'We – er – anticipate that the work will take all of fifteen years, though that is a very rough estimate, you understand. After that time, you may remain on the planet and enjoy the fruits of your labours.'

'I wouldn't be allowed to return to New Earth?'

'No.'

'Then how would I know whether or not the government has fulfilled its promises which you have taken such delight in reciting to me?'

'I feel sure that your friend, the *Hemit Thea Epop Y Us*, could effectively look after the interests of the lands of the Aoidni without much bother.'

The Senator cast a glance at Xenophon who sat ponderously listening to the conversation. Xenophon seemed unyielding.

'What do you say, my Lord Xenophon?' the Duke asked him.

I sense that this business goes far deeper than trade rights and profits . . . far deeper, perhaps, than the Empire itself. Maybe the Duke doesn't feel the fates working in this matter, he thought to himself, but said aloud, 'What is the name of the planet, my Lord?'

The question seemed quite irrelevant. 'Why, it is called *Acima*. It is a strange name, no one seems to know its meaning. It seems quite unconnected with the language of the empire.'

I knew it, Xenophon thought, or at least I should've. Acima! The prospects are unimaginable. I could feel the divine influence behind this affair from the start! 'Then I agree that Senator Androcles should do as you ask. As you say, my Lord, I am quite capable of looking after the affairs of these lands.'

Thoughts rushed through Cheiron's mind, collided with each other, rushed on . . . 'I – I am not sure, my Lord. Permit me to consider the matter. Xenophon seems quite convinced that I should go, but I feel that my friend's motives will have to be discussed in private. Do you have to report to the Magnate?'

'I shall have to hand in a report of the death of General Machaerus and the defeat of the Peacemakers, with certain details omitted of course. Is there communications equipment nearby?'

'We can salvage a transceiver from one of the stratospheres, I daresay.'

'Good. I shall have five days after handing in my report to go over the details with you if you should accept the offer.'

'I will have some wine brought to us, Cheiron,' said Xenophon, relaxing.

'Have some yourselves, by all means. I think I'll go and enjoy the celebrations with my men.' And with that, he stood up, stretched his aching limbs and walked tiredly out of the hut into the flame-flecked darkness.

The Lords of the Zodiac

Cheiron awoke to find the whore snoring at his side. The place stank of wine, a smell that was so sweet the night before. He pulled himself out of the bed and winced as the harsh sunlight struck his eyes through the open door of the ramshackle hut.

Cheiron looked around for his clothes and found them underneath a pile of furs and blankets. He hurriedly dressed and went out of the hut. He crossed the dusty road and made his way to the council hut where he had left Xenophon and the Duke the previous night.

Xenophon and Duke Dolophious were engaged in small talk in the council hut. The Duke had been given some fresh clothes of Aoidni manufacture which contrasted sharply with the fine jewellery on his hands. Xenophon was wearing his sun-blankets but not his veil and turban. They both seemed in good spirits.

'Good morning,' Cheiron said as he closed the door behind him.

'Ah, good morning Senator Androcles,' the Duke greeted him, rising from his chair.

Xenophon raised his hand to his friend.

'I trust that you slept well, my Lord Duke Dolophious.'

'I didn't sleep much, but what there was, was good. I'd like to recover that communications equipment this morning.'

'Very well, I'll order you a detail of men to assist you. You know how to repair a transceiver, my Lord?'

'Just about, I should think. What do you intend to do today?'

'I shall talk things over in detail with Xenophon and I may even come to my final decision.'

They breakfasted and then Cheiron hurried away to attend to the business of getting a group of men together to go with Duke Dolophious to recover the transceiver from one of the wrecked stratospheres.

When at last they had departed for the canyon, Cheiron returned to the council hut and sat down next to Xenophon.

'What is it that you wish to know, my Lord?' Xenophon asked.

'Many things, old friend. I would like to know why it is that when Dolophious mentioned Acima yesterday you were suddenly quite sure that I should accept his offer.'

Xenophon thought about his reply, sighed and then said: 'It is a complex matter, about which I know little. A Teller might be able to tell you a great deal more about the whole thing, and even then there would be serious inconsistencies. I can only tell you what I know from the point of view of a semi-divine, and that is all.'

'Go on.'

'It is the name *Acima* that is important. It is derived, I believe, from an ancient language of this planet. The language and the people to whom it belonged existed here even before the Apocalypse, and that is all that I know about the people themselves. About their religion, I know a little more. This is where Acima comes in. In the tongue of this ancient race, Acima means something like "the Lord will judge". That is the first thing: an extinct earth race has originated a name which belongs to a completely alien world. And I *can* assure you that these people couldn't have had space travel capabilities of any sort.'

'Could it merely be coincidence that the name of the planet and the ancient name are the same?'

'That is possible, in fact more probable if there were not other evidence than simply a name.' Xenophon reached down into the collar of his undergarments beneath his sun-blankets. He fumbled there for a few moments and then drew out the pendant which he always wore with the signs of the Lords of the Zodiac and his personal title inscribed upon it. He held the heavy disc and its golden chain in his hand. 'The question to ask,' he went on, 'is: to which "Lord" does the ancient name refer? The key is here, inscribed upon this metal disc.'

'The Lords of the Zodiac?'

'That is the key. The door and the lock are to be found on Acima. Notice, though, that there are twelve signs of the Lords of the Zodiac whereas the name of the ancients refers to "Lord" in the singular. There is an explanation for this. The ancients, it seems, worshipped a single omnipotent god. The Tellers possess books from the days long before the Apocalypse and from these they have laboriously gleaned great knowledge over the centuries. Of this knowledge I know very little. I know that there is a mighty struggle which has continued over aeons of time. I know that this struggle is the road to Man's destiny one way or another . . . '

'Who fights this struggle on Man's behalf?'

'On the one hand, the twelve Lords of the Zodiac whose signs are inscribed upon this pendant . . . '

'And on the other?'

'On the other hand, there is a force to match the very Lords of the Zodiac themselves.'

'Which force?'

'Another Lord of the Zodiac . . . the thirteenth sign. I don't know what form this Lord takes, I only know that he or she exists.'

'Is this Lord the single god of the ancients?'

'No. It is misleading to believe that. The books of the ancients reflect garbled accounts of their experiences with extra-terrestrial visitors. However, the contents of certain of the books refer to far greater things, things such as the Lords of the Zodiac and the struggle and this thirteenth god who, to them, was the personified collection of all existing evil.'

'So that this god is fighting to destroy mankind, while the other twelve gods of the Tellers fight to preserve mankind.'

'Evil is a human concept, as is goodness. Mankind is the plaything of the galactic overlords whom the Tellers have called the Lords of the Zodiac. It is impossible for even the Tellers to understand the motives of these gods. We only know that there is basically a fight which is the result of some wrong-doing in the eyes of the Lords of the Zodiac by a Lord of the Zodiac. The wrong-doing itself is a concept of the overlords and, as I have stated, we cannot, as humans and mere mortals, understand the motives of gods.'

'Where does the planet Acima come into all this? What have I to do with this cosmic battle?'

Xenophon put the pendant down on the arm of his chair and dropped back into the furs with a sigh. 'I am convinced that Acima is the world that the legends and stories refer to as the place where the final judgement shall occur. Even the name suggests this, and there is a lot of strange interest in the world expressed by the Tellers that Dolophious spoke of. I feel sure that Acima is the place. I also have a feeling that your own destiny lies with that world. And the Lords of the Zodiac can only guide through their messages in the stars. I read the stars last night as best I could, and it was shown to me what your horoscope is. Aries has shown us the way, Cheiron. Aries is your Lord. Follow him. Follow him to the world called Acima, and there seek out the truth. You have the opportunity to seek out what is best for mankind, avoiding the superfluous man-made concepts such as good and evil. You can have the power to decide whether man follows the twelve or the thirteenth.'

Cheiron was silent as if suddenly struck dumb. The whole thing is so utterly fantastic, he thought, why me? Why Cheiron Androcles? Why not the Magnate himself, the man who wields the power?

Xenophon stood up and clapped his friend on the shoulder. 'It is difficult for the spirit of man to accept, I realise. My mother brought me up to believe . . . '

'Can a mortal accept such colossal responsibilities, Xenophon?'

'Without mortals, Cheiron, there could be no gods, for the mortals are there to do the bidding of the gods. The Zodiacs are the gods of humankind.'

'Who are the gods of the Lords of the Zodiac, and who are their gods?'

'The Lords of the Zodiac are the gods of humanity. Humanity exists within our own galaxy with its empires and confederacies and the like. Who rules the universe? And after that the omniverse? The continuum is infinite both outwardly and inwardly and who knows in which other direction.'

Cheiron touched his friend, putting a hand on his shoulder. 'Thank you, Xenophon. There seems little else to do than follow my destiny as Aries has ordained.'

'Until Acima, then you, like our race, must choose which destiny we follow.'

Castle Creon

Castle Creon, perched atop a cliff of milk-white rock, overlooked the city of Sosipolis, capital of the Grand Duchy of Phistars. The castle was the home of Duke Dolophious Thesprotus, ruler of the Grand Duchy.

Cheiron and the Duke had arrived an hour earlier by means of an entycraft which was still being unloaded. The two men sat by the fireplace in the Duke's Great Hall. The coal crackled in the enormous grate as the wind whistled in the chimney and they sat close to the fire because the size of the hall didn't allow an even flow of heat around the place. They sat on large, cushioned chairs and sipped the warming *pyrrha* from crystal vessels.

Duke Dolophious set his translucent cup down on the arm

of his chair and sighed. His face was crimson in the firelight and ripples of light were reflected up onto his face from the jewels on his hands. The flames imposed shadows in the patterns impressed on his long robe. Cheiron looked at the patterns and saw that they represented large golden snakes with long fangs protruding downwards from each reptilian mouth.

'How were your farewells received on New Earth?' the Duke asked, fidgeting slightly.

'The promises you made softened the blow. I daresay that some of the royals of the Aoidni were glad to see my back.'

The Duke smiled without amusement, slightly intoxicated. 'The price of power, my dear Senator. The men who rule, who make the decisions are loved by few.'

Cheiron looked over his shoulder at the hall. The walls were built of blocks of grey-blue stone on which the shadows danced from the coal fire. There were a few works of art, some tapestries and portraits, but little else decorated the hall. The long, narrow council table of darkly polished wood was pushed to one side to reveal a pattern of intertwined snakes on the rich carpet. There was very little furniture other than the table. There was an incongruous video transceiver tucked in a corner to the left of the black double doors.

'Would you like a man to show you to your room?' the Duke asked.

'Yes, I am rather weary after the trip out from New Earth.'

The Duke flipped open a flap on the arm of his chair and touched one of the several buttons beneath it. He closed the flap and lifted his cup to his lips and gulped the remainder of the pyrrha in it. Shortly afterwards the doors of the hall opened softly.

The man looked like a video projection, standing in the great arched doorway. He wore an ostentatious blue and silver gown, pulled in at the waist by a wide gold belt heavily studded with jewels and various ornaments. His facial hair was plentiful and wavy, decorated with a rich metallic glitter which blended with the colours of his large shoulder-clasps decorated with the Dolophious snake-emblem. His face was framed by the weird head-gear which was an abstract form of the head of a snake, fangs and all. 'Yes, sir?' the man asked, directing the question at the Duke.

'See Senator Androcles to his quarters, please, Talos.'

Talos nodded. The Duke gestured to Cheiron with his hand and Cheiron stood up stiffly, turned and walked to the door.

Talos the butler led Cheiron along a wood-panelled passageway which sloped into the depths of the castle. Eventually, the temperature fell and Cheiron guessed that they were inside the castle rock. They turned a corner and entered a brightly lit corridor with plain white walls. There were doors on either side of the corridor at equal intervals. They turned in at the seventh door along.

'You should find this room comfortable, sir,' Talos said as they entered.

The room was decorated with modern furnishings and fittings. Cheiron thanked Talos and Talos left him alone, shutting the door behind him.

Cheiron crossed the room and operated the viewing panel on the wall. Below the cliff was the city of Sosipolis, bathed in the light of the moons of this planet Teledamus. The houses were mostly very old, like Castle Creon that overlooked them. They were the high dome-shaped houses of the early settlers of the planet. The newer buildings, more rectangular, were clustered in pleasant confusion around the market square where small fires flickered and the vagrants that slept in doorways burnt odorous powders to give them a sleep without cold or coarse stone. The city spilled on to the headlands that stretched like the fingers of a sleeping giant out to sea. White snow was suspended from the tops of invisible mountains, concealed by the magic blanket of distant night.

Cheiron turned from the viewing panel, but left it open. He undressed and climbed on to the couch which was situated to the right of the panel. Cheiron turned out the illuminators and lay down on the couch as the moonlight spilled into the room. He didn't activate the relaxers on the couch, he wanted to think as the world poured into the room . . . *so different from the lands of the Aoidni, this world. What will Acima be like? Serene? Tempestuous? Dark? Light?* . . . He relaxed his alert muscles and let his body drift into the peace of slumber . . .

. . . The morning poured in through the viewing panel. Cheiron kept his eyes shut for a while after he had woken up, half expecting to find himself back in his hut when he opened them.

Having not used the relaxers, the couch was like a magnet when he reached the decision that he would have to get up, pulling his body down into its bottomless sea of comfort.

Despite this, Cheiron managed to raise himself and let the daylight from the panel splash on to his skin. He turned on the sound and the noises of the morning suddenly entered the room. The waves crashed on the beaches and roared up against the rocks as the gulls wheeled and screeched. Against this background, the city began to clatter and Cheiron could hear the distant voices of the market sellers calling cheerfully to one another or ousting an over-sleeping vagrant from one of the doorways.

Cheiron cast a glance at the mountains, and then turned from the panel back into the room. He sighed heavily, yawned and stretched and set about looking for his clothes. He found them on the floor where he had left them the previous night. The robes the Duke had given him looked different in the daylight. The fearsome snakes looked almost friendly.

After dressing, Cheiron left his room and went to the Great Hall where, as he expected, he found Duke Dolophious. The Duke bade him good morning cheerfully and they each took a seat.

'How long do I remain at Castle Creon?' Cheiron asked his host.

'We should have things ready in about three days' time, Senator. Would you care for some breakfast?'

'Yes, please, my Lord.'

'Anything in particular?'

'Anything you say.'

Talos was ordered to fetch the breakfast, which the two men heartily consumed, while in between mouthfuls the Duke explained the origin of the food which they were eating.

'Could we discuss Acima, my Lord?' Cheiron asked as two maidservants cleared away the breakfast utensils.

'Of course, Senator. There is much you should know about your mission before you actually embark upon it, of course.'

'Well . . . such as?'

The Duke thought. 'Er – where shall I begin? Ah, yes. Crew. Your crew, Senator, will consist of the minimum number of people. Three to be exact, excluding yourself. Three will be enough to fly in a stratosphere and an entycraft. The entycraft will be stored in the hull of the stratosphere. You'll set up a base by converting the 'sphere into living quarters. Thereafter, the entycraft will be your only form of transport.'

'What's the planet like as a whole?'

'That's a big question, Senator.'

'Just the main details . . .'

'Ahhh . . . Acima is 12,562 kilometres in diameter. Its gravity is .98 of New Earth Standard G. The planet revolves about its sun once in every three hundred Standard years, and is for a proportion of that time in a space-warp. The planet is mostly covered by radioactive material of unknown origin, there being tiny pockets of habitable land usually about one hundred kilometres in diameter. The most extensive of these is in the northern hemisphere, 3,286 kilometres from the north pole. (That is where you will be landing.) The atmosphere is impervious to any other form of communications than lasers. This is due to the radioactive and electric energy contained in the atmosphere. This may give rise to quite violent electrical storms on the planet's surface. The seas of the planet are not seriously polluted by radiation since the rainfall precipitated from the sea is capable of supporting plant life. About the plant life and other life-forms we only know what the Tellers divulge, which is very little.'

'When I first went to the lands of the Aoidni, I at least knew what to expect.'

The Duke eyed Cheiron disapprovingly. 'I can tell you no more about human life-forms than I already have. You will have to act as anthropologist too when you arrive.'

Cheiron nodded. 'Looking ahead, what happens when I've finished my work?'

'We'll send out a couple of nice fat cargo ships and land them in the selected area, together with their crews and then just sit tight until the time comes for the transition.'

Cheiron thought, strange how men of New Earth's Empire manipulate their power. The Duke speaks of the planet Acima as though it were inhabited by intelligent mice. How can he be so sure? Why are people always so sure, so invincible? What will I find on Acima? Why are the Tellers so interested in Acima . . . because of what Xenophon was talking about? How can I question the Duke about that? He'd laugh in my face . . . 'My Lord, what of the Tellers?'

The Duke seemed mildly surprised. 'What of them?'

'I mean what about them in relation to Acima?'

'Oh, who can tell? They're a weird bunch, that's for sure. They come and go in their little spacecraft or they travel with freighters. They mostly visit Acima in their own craft. Otherwise they sky-dive from about 170 kilometres up . . . damn brave, I'll give 'em that much.'

Cheiron relaxed in his chair. He doesn't know much about them. I wonder if there are any Tellers in the city . . .

'Your crew arrives this afternoon. They'll be arriving on the day's only flight from one of my colonies right on the other side of the Duchy. They're all good men. I selected them personally, as I did you. I want this thing to work. It'll be up to you to see that you make it work.'

If I fail, the Duke makes life hell for Xenophon. Yes . . . he thought to himself. 'I understand, my Lord,' he replied.

'Good. You'll be able to contact me via an orbiter. The orbiter will visit the planet's orbit at irregular intervals. You'll be able to contact the orbiter using laser communications equipment. I'll be able to provide anything you'll need on Acima within reason and depending on whether or not we can transport it without arousing suspicion in the Confederacy.'

'What if the Confederacy stumble over the planet's secret by accident?'

'That's a possibility. We'll file a claim to the planet once you've safely touched down there, and we'll back it up by force if need be – but it's a delicate matter. I won't use so much force that I make the planet seem all-important and besides if the plan fails, we'll need to maintain our trading alliance with the Confederacy of Planets.'

'I suppose they'd just shield off the space-warp at the other end like they do the Great Belt routes.'

'That is the most obvious possibility, Senator. But it would take time to build up a screen strong enough to deflect a planet. If we are careful, they will suspect nothing and go on paying no attention to Acima.'

'How did you find out about the warp?'

The Duke sighed. 'I don't really know! One day it just showed up on somebody's scanners and then we looked closer and my scientists and I came up with this idea. It was probably one of those million-to-one chances that crop up now and again.'

What was it Xenophon said, Cheiron thought, 'You have the opportunity to seek out what is best for mankind . . . ' A warp that appears out of nowhere and suddenly a golden opportunity falls straight into Dolophious' lap . . . and then in mine?

Sosipolis

Cheiron decided to go to the landing strip on the other side of Sosipolis by way of the city, having little else to do. Talos the butler was commanded by his master the Duke to fly an entycraft from the castle to the landing strip for the return journey.

Cheiron went by way of a rough road, dropping pleasantly down from the castle rock towards the city. Cheiron walked slowly and with a peace of mind he had not enjoyed since he was a child. In the lands of the Aoidni there had been always the shadow of starvation hanging over the people. Now, the responsibility lay with Xenophon. Cheiron couldn't push his concern for the Aoidni instantly aside, but there seemed little point in worrying since he was now hardly in a position to be able to assist Xenophon. As it was, he felt contented at that time, as he walked slowly along the road with the sunlight shining through the elders, and the migletus, laden with fruit, that shaded him overhead.

He walked into the city with a spring in his step. He had been careful in selecting his clothes from the Duke's wardrobe as he wanted to appear and feel completely casual as he wandered the streets of the city.

The city seemed very different when actually inside it. The high, domed houses clustered together, or were staggered randomly along the cobbled streets. They were constructed mostly of the milky white stone found also in the castle rock. The richer houses were built of the same stone as Castle Creon.

Cheiron made up his mind to visit the market place since the other regions of the city seemed to yield little of interest other than from an anthropological or historical point of view, neither of which interested him at the time. He made his way through the winding, rising, falling streets and assured himself that he would eventually find the market place if he kept on walking in the general direction of the city centre. However confident he was of his prowess as a navigator, he was relieved when he saw the first of the rectangular buildings as were characteristic of most recent market places in the Empire.

As he walked along a shaded alleyway which curved steadily towards the pale blue sunlit square with its bustle and multicoloured stalls, he noticed a couple of transporters turn into the alley from the long building on his left which followed the gently curving contour of the alley. Two large, wooden doors grated shut behind the two large vehicles and footsteps died away into the depths of the warehouse. From around the back of the transporters, two children ran chasing a bright red ball over the cobbles. Their sandaled feet clattered past Cheiron and he smiled at them as they hurried by. Their footsteps turned the corner at the other end of the alley and they were gone.

Cheiron continued to walk towards the hubbub of the market place. His view of the square was obstructed by the transporters which rested on their hover-pads at angles across the road. Cheiron walked into the centre of the alley and moved around the front of the foremost of the transporters in order to pass between them. Then, quite suddenly, the motors of the machine screamed into life and the dust on the cobbles spurted from beneath the hover-pads. Cheiron coughed and winced as the dust flew into his eyes. He stepped back quickly, to avoid the transporter as it pulled away, but the thing seemed to follow him and he hadn't fully realised what was happening until he was pinned against the wall of the warehouse with the hulking vehicle looming over him like some great beast against the blue sky with its wispy pinkish clouds. Cheiron leapt to one side, only to be confronted by the second transporter moving off from across the alley. He made a run for it, and for a moment it seemed as though the thing would accelerate and crush him up against the wall. Fortunately for him, there was too little time and he managed to run to the end of the alley in the direction of the square. A voice called from behind him. He turned to see the transport driver hanging from a rectangular gap in his cabin door: 'Hey! Why don't you watch where you're going?' And the man disappeared.

Shortly after he had entered the market place, Cheiron detected a faint, shrill buzzing in the air. It grew slightly louder. He looked up and saw the fuzzy black speck of an entycraft shoot across the sky. He realised that Talos was on his way to the landing strip, and he became aware of the time it had taken him to find his way through the maze of intertwining streets to the market square. He decided that he had a little time left for him to wander around, and the incident with the transporters sank into his memory as an accident.

Cheiron moved with the crowd. He walked past gaily coloured stalls and stopped occasionally to look at things. He had been given twenty Imperials by the Duke which he intended to spend as he doubted whether Imperial currency would be valid on Acima – if indeed the inhabitants used money at all. He purchased a few trinkets and wandered on.

In the corners of the market place were crates and boxes piled high. As Cheiron walked towards the far right hand corner, he noticed a small group of people gathering round an old man who sat on a fur rug draped over one of the boxes. The old man was bald, but his large beard seemed to make up for that. He wore a long and dirty white robe, and several pendants were hung about his neck and shoulders, one of which Cheiron immediately recognised. A Teller, Cheiron thought and walked over to stand with the group.

The old Teller was selling small tubes from a battered wicker tray at his side. Each tube was marked with a sign of one of the Lords of the Zodiac. He seemed to be selling them cheaply. Cheiron pulled off one of the Imperials pinned to his tunic and handed it to the Teller. 'Lord Aries' word, please.'

The Teller searched in the tray and handed him the tube that he required.

'Can you cast me a personal horoscope for tomorrow?' Cheiron asked the Teller.

The Teller gestured with his fingers.

'Fifteen Imperials.'

(Gasps from the crowd.)

The Teller spoke: 'Come here in the morning. I sense fate working within you. Strange . . . great . . . '

Cheiron dropped the money into the old man's hand and pushed his way through the crowd. I must be careful, he thought, I can't let an old man search into my mission, the Duke insists on secrecy. And I also have other reasons . . .

Stratosphere

In the evening, the Duke's table was shared by Cheiron and the three members of his crew. They ate their fill in silence and then sat back in their chairs with their drinks in their hands.

'I must say, your man who was flying the entycraft back from the landing strip gave me a tough time. Twice I thought we'd had it,' said one of the men, a tall, fair man with chiselled features and a bluish hue to his skin.

'That's something coming from you, Aissa,' said another of them. 'You flew battle cruisers, didn't you?'

'We weren't at war this afternoon. I tell you he was flying the 'craft like a maniac,' Aissa insisted.

The Duke grinned and sipped his drink. 'We all like to show off once in a while, Captain Steropes.'

Cheiron looked around the table at the men. The Duke was wearing the half-smile half-grin induced by the wine that flowed so easily at Castle Creon. The Captain, Aissa Steropes, with that strange blueness to his skin, glowered over his cup of wine. He wore the orange uniform of the space fleet together with the red choker around his neck symbolising his rank in the armed forces. There were two others present. One was called Hoples Perseis, the soldier formerly with the Imperial Guard, who had full, bronzed features with a kind of hidden edge to them that was faintly visible in his protruding eyes. Next to Hoples sat the doctor, Iasus Golgos, who wore the uniform of the Imperial Medical Academy. The doctor interested Cheiron most of all. He was a hunched, brooding man. An anachronism. Cheiron recognised the streak of the revolutionary in him that he had within himself. Doctors, as such, were long outdated by the machines, but this man wore the white choker of a doctor together with the uniform of the ancient Imperial Academy.

The silence lasted until Captain Steropes directed a question at the Duke: 'What's the drill for tomorrow, my Lord?'

The Duke set his drink down on the table. 'The starliner you and your companions arrived here on is being refuelled and loaded with the stratosphere for your mission. Tomorrow after breakfast you can all load your personal gear. You, Captain Steropes, can have a look at the stratosphere controls and make all of your primary settings. Doctor Golgos and Centurion Perseis can also go to the 'sphere to prepare the medical equipment . . .' (he looked at the doctor) ' . . . And the 'sphere's weaponry. You may spend the day doing all that you can to the 'sphere under the guidance of Senator Androcles, and then, if you wish, you can go to the city for a night out before returning here for the night. The starliner leaves the day after tomorrow.'

'What's security like around the 'sphere?' Centurion Perseis wanted to know.

'No one is aware of the purpose of the stratosphere, Centurion, except for a few officials. My servants are completely trustworthy as well. In case of the highly unlikely event that an enemy should discover the plan and attempt to sabotage the 'sphere, autoguards have been placed around the starliner.'

The Centurion frowned. 'I don't trust those mechanical efforts. You ought to have men posted on the landing strip.'

'Men's minds can be altered,' the Duke argued. 'Robots are incapable of disloyalty.'

The Centurion shrugged.

'The Empire itself is a machine,' the Doctor put in. 'The Empire is a machine of the ultimate kind. The Empire doesn't trust humans very much at all. I'm sorry if that offends you, my Lord Duke Dolophious.'

The Duke laughed inwardly. 'I am not offended.' Soon I shall have the power of an empire, he thought, the power of an empire! An empire within a man. I shall soon control the empire's access to the Great Belt of Trading Worlds, and the Empire will respect me as it respects the Confederacy of Planets now . . .

As Cheiron lay on his couch that night, he read the contents of the capsule the old man in the market place had sold him earlier. The horoscope was written on a rough piece of dirty paper, but the writing was beautiful, and it was the message that one paid for. Cheiron read . . .

> 'Over-confidence is a danger lurking close by. Don't let others blind you to the truth with false securities.

A forthcoming journey may bring some surprises . . .
but they may not all be pleasant.

Lord Aries has spoken to: the Teller Nominus.'

After reading the message through a number of times, Cheiron slipped it back into the tube and turned out the room's illumination. Moonlight flooded the room and Cheiron fell asleep holding the tube in his palm.

The next morning, after breakfast, they went to the landing strip. Aissa Steropes insisted on flying the entycraft to avoid a repeat of his experiences with Talos as pilot the day before.

As the entycraft swiftly descended to the ribbon of gravel stretching away into the distance, the size of the starliner astounded Cheiron. He had never seen a starliner other than in orbit around a planet, where there was little to relate its true size to.

The starliner was about eight hundred metres high and seemed utterly out of place because of its gigantic size. It consisted of four silver columns clustered tightly together. The sides were lined with long rows of video-scopes for the viewing panels. About half-way up one of the columns facing the entycraft as it came in was a rectangular hatch about fifty metres high and as wide as the column, which was about a hundred metres in diameter. The columns were each emblazoned with the Dolophious serpent, and the hatch door was occupied by the fearsome head of one of these. The starliner was supported by an equally massive launch and debarcation gantry and its specially fitted rocket-launch motors were half immersed in a giant water container which had been cut into the solid rock bed of the landing strip.

The strip itself was otherwise empty but for a rickety shack some way off. The landing strip was surrounded by open ground which was barren and wind blown.

The entycraft made contact with the gravel which hissed as it shifted under the 'craft's legs. The two cockpit domes swung open and the sunlight gleamed on the tinted transparencies. The passengers and pilot jumped to the ground from within. They squinted and shaded their eyes to look up towards the top of the starliner as it soared high above them. It seemed to move towards them as the clouds moved overhead.

After a time, Captain Steropes clapped his hands together and their eyes were dragged away from the awesome spectacle. 'Time we got started,' he said and walked towards the steps leading on to the gantry stack. They all followed, pointing and talking about the gargantuan at whose feet they stood.

They made their way to the control housing of the gantry and were confronted by an autoguard. Its electron torch swivelled to point at them. Cheiron showed it his identi-card and the others did the same as they walked past the guard and entered the control housing.

Cheiron walked to the transceiver on one of the control panels and made contact with the starliner's flight deck. The video screen jumped and flashed into life and the picture cleared to reveal the face of the 'liner's master. 'Permission to come aboard, sir,' Cheiron requested.

'Permission granted, Senator,' the voice replied.

They walked to the elevator on the other side of the room and climbed into the cage. There was a loud hiss and then the elevator lurched upwards. The ceiling opened and then snapped shut as the cage swept upwards to the boarding tube. This they quickly crossed and entered the starliner itself.

The ship's master greeted them cordially in the corridor. He led them through numerous luxurious corridors, padded with soft ochre material and illuminated by gentle light which shone from small reliefs in the wall padding. There were no 'roof' or 'floor' to a passageway as they were uniformly padded all around.

They were led to the starliner's main elevator where they left the captain standing in the corridor and were whisked downwards. The elevator jostled as it crossed over into a different shaft and then after a few seconds and two hundred metres more it slowed down and came to a halt with a gentle thud.

The doors of the elevator slid aside and they left the plush interior of the lift and stepped out on to solid deck plates.

'Sweet, sweet home,' said the Doctor as he looked up at the giant orb of the stratosphere. It was suspended from the launching bay by cables and purring, crackling repeller rays directed at the stratosphere from the deck and walls. Long balconies curled around the 'sphere and technicians in their grey uniforms fussed over the 'sphere like insects. But the 'sphere seemed to be smiling as it reflected its surroundings on its bright red hull.

One of the technicians came across the deck towards the group of men. From somewhere above a laser crackled and sparked and some obscure part of the 'sphere's anatomy was connected to the rest of the body. The technician carried four shiny objects in his arms. He handed the four men one each. 'You'll need these if you're going near the stratosphere – protection caps.'

They pulled the caps over their heads and followed the man beneath the stratosphere to the single leg that protruded down from one of the four hatches, with the elevator tube standing vacant at the bottom of the leg.

They were soon whisked on to the flight deck. The deck was dimly illuminated as the viewing panels were turned off. Aissa Steropes walked across to the pilot's console and eased himself into the chair. He ran his fingers over the controls to get the feel of them and then activated the viewers. The scene outside cast its light in on the flight deck and the men moved forward to have a closer look at the controls of their craft. The Captain touched a row of buttons and the pictures on each viewing panel became unrelated. One showed the elevator leg, another the scene directly in front of the craft . . . 'All round vision,' the Captain reported needlessly and more to himself than anyone else. 'Can't be bad,' he remarked.

They left the Captain testing the controls of the stratosphere and walked about, exploring the ship's laboratory, sick bay and living accommodation which they found to their satisfaction. The Duke had obviously spent a great deal of time and Imperials on furnishing the stratosphere for their mission and they realised how much this mission meant to the Duke.

Soon, cables and two elevator shafts drooped down the side of the starliner to the ground. A few hundred metres away from the liner, a group of frustrated technicians shifted a target that the Centurion had set up to make adjustments to the 'sphere's x-ray laser which he fired out of the open hatchway.

Cheiron directed his crew in their work so that by the time they had completed what they wanted to do that day, the stratosphere was looking just as Cheiron wanted it. He even went as far as having the Dolophious serpent emblem removed from the hull so that there was no risk of frightening the natives of the planet Acima with the fearsome creature.

When the day's work was completed, it was night, lit only by the moon. The four men stood on the edge of the open hatchway and looked out at the stars and Castle Creon in the distance, and the city of Sosipolis with music tinkling from its buildings. They breathed the cool night air and it seemed as though they could stand in the hatchway for ever and watch time pass by.

'What exactly happens tomorrow?' Cheiron asked the Captain.

Aissa leant against the side of the hatchway and folded his arms, looking at the sky. 'When we leave, you mean? Well, the starliner takes us to Acima and they simply drop us from a few hundred kilometres into the atmosphere. If they do the thing right, when I activate the repellers we should be on course for our landing spot, falling at a steep angle so that we don't stray into the radiation zone. Then we choose a landing site and touch down. They'll be watching us down with lasers as we fall. Then, after we've landed, hopefully in one piece, well . . . the next move'll be ours to make.'

A voice boomed from somewhere behind them: 'Okay with you two fellows if we close the store for the night, now?'

They turned. A technician stood on the balcony on the other side of the bay, dwarfed by the size of the place. They could just see his dark shape by the stratosphere.

'Okay,' Cheiron said and they walked towards the elevator in the opposite wall of the launching bay.

'You going to the city tonight?' Cheiron asked the others.

'You bet. I want to get me a last survey of a female before we go in search of the women of Acima,' Hoples replied.

'Me too,' said the Doctor.

The Captain nodded.

They climbed into the elevator and it hissed away into the depths of the starliner as the giant hatch slowly clanked shut and the moonlight was shielded out. The autoguards spilled out on to the deckplates.

The Devil

They scrunched across the gravel away from the starliner towards the entycraft with its aero-domes still flung open. The entycraft would be coming with them to Acima also and it was their task the next morning to load the entycraft into the stratosphere.

Now, as they approached the craft, Centurion Perseis noticed a black form hanging from the open right hand cockpit of the entycraft. 'What's that?' he hissed, pointing out the object.

All four halted and fell silent. The shape did not move.

'Let's split up and move towards it slowly,' Hoples Perseis said, and they did so.

The Doctor was the first to reach the entycraft and the others were only seconds behind. They found the Doctor cradling an old man in his lap after pulling the body down from where it hung on the 'craft. Cheiron recognised him instantly as the old Teller from the market place the previous day. A cool breeze blew, ruffling their hair. The Doctor looked up at them.

'Dead?' Cheiron asked.

'Throwing-knife in the back,' the Doctor reported. 'Neat throw, too. Straight into the heart.'

'Pretty acurate,' Hoples agreed. 'Anybody know who he is?'

'He was a Teller,' Cheiron said. 'I bought a horoscope from him yesterday in the market place. He was going to make a personal horoscope out for me.'

'Who'd want to kill a Teller?' Aissa wanted to know.

'Autoguards don't carry throwing-knives,' Hoples said with a hint of humour in his voice.

The Captain looked down at the face, the grey beard and the lipless mouth and the glazed eyes as innocently wide open as they were when the blade struck the old man from behind. 'Maybe he was bringing your horoscope . . . hotly pursued by somebody who didn't want you to have it. Anything special about your horoscope, Senator?'

Shall I tell them? . . . No. 'I'll never know now.'

'We hope,' the Doctor said, wiping the blood from his hand on to the Teller's robe. 'He hasn't been dead too long, probably just after nightfall. What'll we do with him?'

'Turn him over to the city authorities, I suppose,' Cheiron said.

They loaded the body into the baggage compartment of the entycraft and then climbed into the cockpit. The dust whirled and the wings began to move and the entycraft buzzed away into the moonlit sky. Their night out in the city was postponed by the authorities who were very thorough in their questioning and it took a special message from Duke Dolophious to set them free.

By the time they returned to Castle Creon, it was early morning and they all decided to go straight to bed and get as much sleep as possible in readiness for the following day.

Cheiron went to his room and undressed. He crawled on to his couch and was about to activate the relaxers when he noticed a small tube resting on the table near the couch. He propped himself up and reached out and grabbed it. It was similar to the container his horoscope had been inside yesterday. He opened it, expecting to find the horoscope that he had ordered and paid the money for. The paper, however, contained a brief warning: 'BEWARE THE FOLLOWERS OF THE THIRTEENTH SIGN' and that was all.

It can only mean the Thirteenth Lord of the Zodiac, Cheiron thought, the anonymous Thirteenth Lord.

Thoughts rushed turbulently through his mind for about an hour, and then he put the tube back on to the table and activated the relaxers.

Cheiron slept peacefully for some time . . . then the dream came to him quite suddenly out of the darkness. There was a door, a plain door surrounded by blackness. He was led to the door by a big man with the head of a ram that had human eyes. There was no sound. The man indicated the door and Cheiron opened it. There was bright yellow light. There was a thing coiled on the floor, sleeping. It awoke suddenly. The snake uncoiled and lashed up at his face. The fangs sank into his cheek and then he lay in the yellow light trembling, his eyes glazed as if in death and sweat dripping from him as indescribable pain wracked his body. The door to the room closed slowly. It closed and the light narrowed in the crack of the door, and then . . . he was awake. Sleep had fled suddenly and his eyes were wide open, his senses alert. The door of his own room was opening slowly, and yellow light from the corridor flowing in and slipping over his face. He gripped the couch to make sure that he was awake. It was tangible. He narrowed his eyes and saw something glint in the doorway. The latch clicked as a hand released it. Cheiron began to sweat as the gap widened and a large figure stood silhouetted in the doorway.

Cheiron tried to make out the form's identity, but it was impossible. He was just a dark outline against the brightness of the corridor. Something glinted again in the man's right hand. He moved forward towards the couch. Cheiron steadied his breathing and tried to look and sound as though he was sleeping, without fully closing his eyes. He heard the relaxers purring and wondered how he was awake . . . The man halted at the foot of the couch and levelled the black object in his hand to point directly at Cheiron's head. Cheiron's hand stabbed the control box next to the couch. He hit the viewing-panel button and moonlight flowed into the room. The man gasped and jumped. Cheiron's foot flew up and struck the thing in his hand and his startled nerves caused the man to release it. Cheiron jumped from the couch and the two of them rolled over on the floor. The man broke free and dived for the object Cheiron had kicked from his hand, but Cheiron dragged him back and made a bid for the thing himself. He felt powerful hands grab his thighs and pull at him, but he managed to grab the thing. The next thing he knew, the hands were at his throat and squeezing. Cheiron choked and found that he couldn't breathe. The viewing panel blurred in his vision. He fumbled with the weapon to find the correct way of holding it. Almost unconscious, he touched what he hoped was the firing stud. There was a spitting sound, a shriek of pain, and the grip around Cheiron's throat relaxed.

Cheiron pushed the body off him. He lay on the floor trying to recover his breath for a long time, the weapon held limply in his hand. The sweat was cold on his body.

At last, Cheiron managed to get up. He walked to the control box, massaging his throat gingerly, and illuminated the room. He saw the trembling body of Talos the butler at the foot of the couch. There was something stuck in the butler's neck. Cheiron remembered the weapon and looked down at it in his hand. He put it down on the couch. He deactivated the relaxers and sat down on the couch himself. Lord Aries saved my life, he thought, there is no other explanation for it. The man in the dream with the ram's head . . . I thank you, my Lord Aries.

After the fire in his throat relented slightly, Cheiron went to the door and called out. Footsteps came running. The Duke and the three crewmen entered the room as Cheiron pulled on his gown and fastened it.

'Talos!' the Duke breathed.

The Doctor knelt by the side of the butler and found the dart in his neck.

'He tried to kill me,' Cheiron said, looking at the questioning faces. He picked up the weapon from the couch. 'With this.'

'He obviously failed,' Hoples Perseis remarked.

'I managed to kick it from his hand. We struggled and I got

hold of the thing. He tried to strangle me and I pressed the firing stud . . .'

The Doctor stood up and looked at Cheiron's neck. He touched the bruises softly. 'Looks like he nearly succeeded,' he said. He took the weapon from Cheiron's hand and looked at it. He handed it to the Centurion. 'What do you make of this?'

The Centurion examined it closely, then reported: 'Simple assassin's hypodermic dart gun. What was in the hypo-dart?'

'Plutonium. About .005 of a gramme. He'll die of a cancer within two Standard days.'

Cheiron remembered the transporters in the alleyway, then the message tube and the old Teller; BEWARE THE FOLLOWERS OF THE THIRTEENTH SIGN.

'I thought that all your servants were trustworthy,' said Hoples.

'I – I can't think what possessed him to do such a thing . . . Talos has been with me for years. Who could've stolen his loyalty?'

The Thirteenth Lord, perhaps, Cheiron thought. He knelt down beside Talos and looked at the man, shaking his head.

Talos murmured softly: 'The Devil has taken my soul!'

Cheiron frowned. The Devil? He noticed something gleaming on Talos's gown. A circular pendant lay on his chest. Cheiron motioned towards it and Talos gripped his hand. Cheiron pulled Talos's hand away and took hold of the pendant. He tugged at it and the chain snapped around Talos's neck. They all crowded round.

'Some local deity?' the Doctor asked, looking at the lizard-like creature on the pendant. Its head was almost human, but predominantly reptilian but its hands and feet were humanoid. It stood erect on two legs and clutched an ornate trident in its left hand.

'Most likely,' Cheiron said, thinking, I'll not tell them about the Thirteenth Lord yet. This may be him. He looked closely at the creature on the pendant. It had cruel eyes and a reptile's mouth that seemed to contain human teeth.

'I've never come across anything like that on this world,' the Duke said.

The Doctor sighed. 'Nothing much that I can do for this poor blighter, but put him out of his misery for good.'

'Let him suffer!' the Duke rasped, suddenly angry at the treachery.

'I let no man suffer, my Lord,' the Doctor retorted crisply. 'I suggest that you encase his body in something dense like lead and bury it deep. In a short time his body will become radioactive.' With that, the Doctor went out of the room to fetch his equipment.

'It's lucky you weren't using your relaxers, Senator,' the Duke remarked.

Cheiron stood up. 'Yes – yes it is. By the way, I found the tube.'

'Good. Some fellow in the city wanted you to have it. Any connection with this business?'

'Er – no, no connection.' Cheiron looked at the pendant in his hand. 'I think I'll hang on to this,' he said, and pushed it into the pocket of his robe.

'D'you think it was Talos who killed the old Teller?' Aissa asked Cheiron.

'Perhaps, or maybe some other of these "Devil" worshippers.'

'I'll have them all routed out and transported to some less hospitable colony!' the Duke proclaimed.

'They may not all be responsible,' Cheiron said. 'There are fanatics among the followers of any creed.'

'Pah! I'm going to bed. I'll send some servants down to deal with the body.' The Duke turned to the door and walked quickly away.

The Doctor returned with his bag and Talos was soon quite dead. The servants came and carried the body away, and the Doctor went along with them to make sure that the body was properly disposed of.

When they had all returned to their beds, Cheiron sat down on the edge of the couch and pondered over the pendant he had taken from Talos. After a time he stretched out on the couch and slept lightly, without the relaxers.

Starliner

The hatch within a hatch yawned. The entycraft entered the starliner, then the stratosphere, and came to rest on its legs as the loud buzz of the wings died away. The launching bay hatch slammed to and shut out the daylight. The cockpit domes opened and four men jumped out. The entycraft creaked as the men left it.

'Let's get the entycraft secure,' the Captain said and they set about latching the domes shut and anchoring the legs of the entycraft to the floor of the tiny launch bay of the stratosphere.

Minutes later, they sat secure in their contour chairs as the time for the lift-off of the starliner drew nearer.

Shortly before lift-off, the ship's master spoke to them over the transceiver. 'You all secure down there?' he asked.

'All secure, sir,' the Captain replied.

'Anything else you'll be needing before we blast off, Senator Androcles?'

'No, thanks. Is the Duke coming along to see us off?'

'I believe he's coming aboard now. You'll be able to come up to the flight deck once we're in orbit. We won't be entering hyper-space until a half hour after blast off.'

'Thank you.'

The transceiver was lifeless again.

The Captain glanced around at his companions. He smiled. 'All strapped in for the big event?'

They all nodded. Cheiron glanced around the flight deck of the stratosphere. Hoples Perseis sat in the co-pilot's chair and rested his big hands on the control panel. The Doctor relaxed in his chair and stared into the lights that blinked on his own panel. Cheiron sat in the passenger chair. He felt the pendant on his chest underneath his uniform.

A few minutes passed, then a woman's voice sounded on the transceiver: 'Good morning, ladies and gentlemen. I would like to welcome you aboard on behalf of Captain Cedalion and his crew and hope that you find the journey comfortable. Blast-off will be in two minutes' time. Will you all please secure yourselves until we are in orbit. Thank you.'

It seemed an eternity before the rocket motors rumbled into life. The rumble built up into a terrific roar and vibrations shook the starliner from nose to stern. The four men in the stratosphere felt their bones rattle as the vibration reached them. They felt a sudden lurch and then a surge of intense power beneath them as the liner lifted away from the ground. The forces of gravity pushed them into their seats as repeller rays fought to cancel the effect of acceleration down to a minimum. The starliner climbed higher. The roar of the rocket motors relented, giving way to a rasping throb. Then, once again the sound built up and vibrations racked the ship again. Then the noise and the vibration slowly died away and there was hissing . . . then silence. The gravity forces fled and the four of them sighed with relief.

The woman again: 'You may now relax. We will be firing out of orbit in a few minutes' time. We will be coming up to the space-warp in twenty minutes and you will be informed when that time comes. Thank you.'

Cheiron unfastened his safety belt and walked to the Captain's console. He activated the transceiver. 'Where do I find the Duke?'

The master's voice returned: 'Up here on the flight deck, Senator. Feel free to come up here if you so wish.'

'Thanks.' He turned off the transceiver. 'Anyone coming along to take leave of Duke Dolophious?'

They all shook their heads.

Cheiron left the stratosphere and went by way of the elevator up to the flight deck.

The Duke stood behind the pilot and co-pilot, looking out of the enormous viewing panel. The flight deck was illuminated only by the instrument panels and the light from the great blue-green hemisphere which occupied most of the viewing panel.

'I hope that you were comfortable on the way up, Senator,' the Duke said to Cheiron as the door slid shut behind him.

'As comfortable as I expected to be, thank you, sire. That was quite an experience.' Cheiron turned to the Duke. 'I don't suppose we'll be meeting again after we drop.'

'Don't tell me this is a fond farewell. Ah – we're breaking orbit.'

'I just want your word that you'll fulfil your promises concerning the lands of the Aoidni.'

'You have it, Senator.'

Repellers hummed and the planet in the viewing panel rapidly decreased in size.

As they approached the great wound in the continuum of space, the pilot began to sweat in anticipation. He finished his calculations and inserted them into the auto pilot. He craned forwards but there was nothing to see. Then the starliner fell into the warp. Stars reappeared and cascaded. They soared away and leaped past, the constellations contorted. The ship seemed to be spinning . . . then the stars came to rest and the pilot breathed a sigh of relief.

'Beautifully executed, Captain,' the Duke said. 'How long to Acima?'

'Ten minutes or so.'

The Duke looked at Cheiron. 'You'd better return to the 'sphere, Senator. Don't worry about the lands of the Aoidni; I am always true to my word.'

Cheiron nodded. 'You'll be watching us down to Acima?'

'Yes, with interest,' the Duke replied.

Cheiron nodded again and turned towards the door.

The Duke folded his arms and looked out into space.

PART TWO: THE PEOPLE ON THE HILL

The Valley

The viewing panels were activated. The launching bay lay in half-light. Empty. Shadows.

Aissa switched a panel to rear view. The planet Acima's northern hemisphere was framed in the hatchway to the launching bay. It was strange to think that the previous night they had been standing in that hatchway. Now they sat in the twilight, strapped into their contour chairs with seconds only to wait before they finally embarked on their adventure.

There was nervous silence but for the hissing of the transceiver.

'Stand by,' the voice cut the still air. 'Ten seconds and counting.'

'All is well here,' Captain Steropes returned.

More silence.

'Six . . . five . . . four . . . three . . . two . . . one . . .'

Repeller rays sparkled blue in the vacuum.

'. . . Zero!'

The starliner was falling away into space, the silver metal glinting in the light reflected from the planet.

From the flight-deck of the starliner, the Duke looked on as the bright red orb rotated slowly, falling downwards into the immense purple-blue with the tiny laser flashing on its hull.

For a long time, the silence persisted. Then there was a rushing sound and bright orange shot from the corners of the viewing panels as the stratosphere entered the atmosphere of the planet.

The transceiver was crackling loudly. Aissa switched it off and quickly turned his eyes back to his instruments. He watched the altimeter drop and rested his finger on a red button close by. Then, he depressed the button hard. The stratosphere jolted and there was a sudden hum. The repellers protested violently against the force of gravity on the stratosphere. They could see the clouds, now stretching to the wavering horizon. Aissa persisted with the repellers. The altimeter began to fall more steadily as Aissa brought the stratosphere under control.

They sighed with relief and let out exclamations as the stratosphere skimmed the cloud layers under Aissa's expert guidance.

'Well done, friend,' Hoples commented.

'Don't feel relieved yet. The scanners are showing an electrical storm of some violence below the cloud.'

'Must we go through it?' Cheiron asked.

'If we go around it we'll overshoot the landing area and enter the radiation zone. Besides, there's too much pressure on the repellers due to our rate of fall to give us much room for manoeuvre. At least if we go through the storm we won't fall like a stone.'

The stratosphere broke through the clouds and was suddenly gripped by an invisible force and flung from side to side. There was only enough time to see that there was land below and then the horizon rolled away. Aissa tried to force the stratosphere to flow along with the air currents smoothly by banking, but the storm was erratic and the 'sphere fell down and was forced suddenly upwards, then down again. Aissa rolled the stratosphere downwards and tried to force the craft out of the turbulence. But the storm picked up the 'sphere and flung it with all its might. Aissa wrestled to bring the 'sphere under control. Hoples joined him in the attempt. Then there was a thunderclap, followed by a loud bang. The stratosphere leaped and jolted. Black smoke billowed around the viewing panels, and was dispersed by the wind and rain. The angry whining of the repellers stopped.

'What's happening?' the Doctor yelled over the sound of the wind and rain.

'Lightning!' Hoples replied, 'We've been hit.'

'The repellers have shorted out!' Aissa shouted, 'I'll have to let the storm carry us and then try to glide her in . . .'

'What about the entycraft?' Cheiron asked loudly.

'Weather's too rough, the 'craft'd be smashed to pieces in seconds.'

'You can't glide a 'sphere!' the Doctor pointed out.

'What else can I damn well do?'

'I'll go down and get us some power from the repellers,' the Doctor suggested.

'No harm in trying. Senator, go with the Doctor. See what you can do. Just a single repeller could save us.'

The two men slipped and stumbled their way to the door. The Doctor opened it and let gravity slam him into the elevator as the stratosphere rolled. It rolled again and the Doctor had to pull Cheiron up into the elevator.

The elevator took them down into the bowels of the stratosphere. As they left it they were suddenly hit by a wave of smoke. Somewhere in the dark sparks flared giving a faint illumination. The smoke blended into the darkness and made their eyes run.

'Look for the toolkit,' Cheiron gasped.

They both groped in the swirling, tumbling darkness.

'I've got it!' the Doctor called.

They pulled their way along to the place where the sparks seemed to originate. Cheiron ripped away a buckled plate and looked inside, seeing flames burning. They found an extinguisher in the toolkit and blasted the heart of the fire. The flames died away to reveal a blackened mess.

'Is there a torch in the kit?' Cheiron asked.

The Doctor sorted through, then found one and illuminated the machinery.

'It looks like a valve is broken. Without it the repellers might overheat.'

'At the moment they're not working at all,' the Doctor argued. He pulled a tool from the kit and fiddled about for a short while. Suddenly the repellers hummed into life.

The two men slowly and with difficulty made their way back to the flight deck. Both were relieved to be back in their contour chairs.

'We've survived the worst of it – the storm seems to be clearing. We're over a valley. The population seems to be concentrated on a large industrial complex on the riverside. Doctor, would you confirm that impression?'

The Doctor looked at the reports from the scanners. 'There

are chemical concentrations in the air which appear to be unnatural. They must be emanating from this industrial area. There is much vegetation, and a normal radiation level in this part of the valley. It's early morning here, but no humans are moving about.'

Cheiron interrupted: 'Good. I don't want to frighten them with our arrival.'

'They seem more advanced than we had expected,' Hoples said. 'That industrial place covers twenty square kilometres.'

'It would be best to land now,' Aissa said.

'Our makeshift repairs won't last forever,' Cheiron agreed.

The stratosphere dropped to a height of about sixty metres and flew horizontally over the river. Aissa banked left and flew west for seven or eight hectometres until they flew low over hilly ground.

'There's a village on this hill,' the Doctor reported.

Aissa took the stratosphere higher.

'It's empty, no people at all. I think this is as good a place as any . . .'

The stratosphere angled down and Aissa extended the legs. The 'sphere touched down on the edge of a hill overlooking a cliff-like drop of sandstone which fell for about twelve metres. The great red stratosphere loomed over the lush green scenery.

The stratosphere was motionless on its legs, its repellers silent. Then, the elevator tube descended and the four men stepped out on to the coarse grass of the wild hill. A cold, wet wind blew over them. They walked from beneath the stratosphere and stood on the edge of the sandstone outcroppings at the top of the sheer drop. They looked for the river. It lay at some distance, but its line was apparent. It flowed into the depths of the strange industrial complex, dark and brooding and belching multicoloured smoke. Separating the hill on which they stood from the black building, if it could be called that, was an area of rough ground, thinly scattered with trees. A tall bank rose up beyond, with a forbidding gateway giving entrance beneath it. The complex was vast and had great towers and chimney stacks with giant buildings encrusted with grime. Hissing, clanking and roaring noises issued from it. It was cut short just after a rough road disappeared into it after running parallel to, though some distance away from, the murky, shallow river. The complex gave way to green fields and trees which spread gently over to another area of high ground covered with trees about a kilometre distant. The trees spread everywhere and staggered away northwards growing denser as they went. There were hills in the distance and the watery blue haze shrouded them, drawing the eye to a milky sky overcast with clouds heavily laden with water.

They breathed the fresh air from the rocks and stood in silence until the Doctor asked: 'Well, gentlemen, what do you make of all that?'

Orbiter

Duke Dolophious looked on as the master of the starliner delicately adjusted the controls of an observer. The master sat up and shook his head. 'I've lost them. The last information we received was that the craft was being shaken about and then it shot out of our beam. With the instruments on my ship we wouldn't stand much chance of finding them down there.'

'I know, Captain,' the Duke sighed. 'Head for the nearest base. An orbiter will have to search them out.'

The master opened the correct channel and began talking into the transceiver.

'You say that human beings couldn't live in there, Doctor Golgos?' Cheiron asked, indicating the industrial site.

'Too much pollution at groundlevel for the air to sustain life in there,' the Doctor replied.

'What do you think happened to the people in that village we flew over?' Aissa asked Cheiron.

The Senator scratched his head. 'I've no idea, yet. I had better do a little exploring today.'

'Not alone, though,' Hoples broke in. 'I think it wise that we travel in groups or pairs in case of attack.'

'I don't want us to look heavily armed, though,' Cheiron said to him.

'One torch per pair should be enough,' Hoples stipulated.

‘One man can communicate with the natives while the other stands ready to defend,’ the Doctor chuckled.

‘That sounds reasonable,’ Cheiron agreed.

Aissa turned and looked up at the stratosphere. ‘We ought to carry out repairs before we consider excursions away from the ’sphere.’

They began to walk back towards the stratosphere. Once inside they went to their living quarters and set about clearing up and preparing themselves for travel.

Hoples and Aissa set about making more permanent repairs in the engine room while the Doctor and Cheiron made a preliminary survey outside. They looked at the soil at several points around the ship and took samples of vegetation. They noted the numerous varieties of birds and took some video film. But neither ventured more than fifty metres from the stratosphere; neither of them was armed.

At noon they returned, glad to be inside and warm again. It was obviously summer, but it seemed doubtful if the temperature could ever reach a tropical level.

They sat around the table in the ship’s kitchen and ate in silence until they had finished. Cheiron stood up and gathered up the utensils. He walked to a disposal unit and pushed them into it. The machine gulped hungrily.

The Doctor leant back in his chair. ‘How long will our supplies last?’ he asked.

‘About ten days,’ Hoples replied.

‘Then what?’ Cheiron asked.

‘The Duke seemed to be under the impression that we make contact with the natives and obtain food from them,’ Aissa said.

‘So far we haven’t even glimpsed any “natives”,’ Hoples countered.

‘Maybe we’re lucky not to have done,’ the Doctor suggested. ‘They may not be friendly.’

Cheiron was silent, thoughtful, while the others joked about the possible nature of Acima’s inhabitants. His was a serious and peaceful mission. He was a man of action, and itched to begin.

‘I wish to make a survey in the entycraft,’ Cheiron said.

‘I’m agreeable,’ Aissa said. ‘Providing you take someone along with you.’

‘I’ll go,’ the Doctor volunteered.

The Doctor and Cheiron checked the entycraft and found

that it was undamaged by the ferocity of the storm. Soon, the entycraft was high over the valley with Cheiron at the controls. He kept the craft at a high level so that those below couldn't recognise it as a flying machine, and might mistake it for a bird, due to the peculiar action of the wings. Most of the time, he made it glide on the air currents.

They followed winding, rough roads for about seven kilometres until the entycraft was flying over a small village community in among the hills. The focal point was a massive, ornate building in a roughly central position in relation to the village. It was constructed of sandstone and completely dominated the entire area. It had an arch which looked to be about fifteen metres high and enclosed a vast, multicoloured transparency. This did not seem to be designed for any practical purpose. It was apparently decorative, bearing designs and colouration, but from their altitude the only way of achieving a close look was through a video-scope.

The people of the village lived in small dwellings of wattle and daub and cultivated the land for food. Most activity seemed to be concentrated on the land in front of the great building. There seemed far too many people, however, for the accommodation of the village to be adequate.

It was late afternoon when the entycraft headed back towards the stratosphere perched on the hill. They landed the 'craft a short distance from the stratosphere on a slope and left it there for convenience.

When he had finished describing their flight to Aissa and Hoples, Cheiron went outside and stood alone on one of the rocks, looking out at the flat, gentle land between the hill and the other area of high ground. The wind sang in his ears as he watched the dusk gather on the faraway hills. Through the cloud, the sun was shooting long, golden rays across the landscape, putting a yellow on the black of the ugly industrial building as the smoke poured from it into the atmosphere from tall chimneys.

Cheiron stood there for a long time contemplating the events of the past days. Suddenly he had been flung over to the other side of the galaxy, away from his home in the lands he had helped to liberate and now he stood on a hillside in a new world. It seemed so incredible that his mind didn't seem to want to accept what had transpired. It was almost like a dream.

He put his hand beneath his shirt and ran his thumb over

the pendant illustrating the mysterious Devil-god. He was deep in thought, wondering about the pendant when something on the hill in front of him caught his eye. It was some time before his mind registered it. When the realisation of movement struck him he glanced up. From out of the trees, a long thread of people was emerging and coming across the flat area.

The missing villagers! Cheiron thought. They're returning. I'd better –

'Cheiron!' somebody shouted.

Cheiron turned and saw the Doctor standing just outside of the elevator tube.

'They've sent an orbiter to look for us. There's a laser transmission coming through now.'

'There are some people crossing the land down there!' Cheiron called back.

The Doctor looked towards the hill. 'You're right! I'll just report it to the others. Will you stay there and watch them?'

'I won't let them out of my sight,' Cheiron promised. 'Go and tell the Duke that we're about to make our first contact. I think they've spotted the stratosphere.'

The Doctor waved and went back to the lift tube. It shot up into the stratosphere.

Cheiron watched the people approach, raggedly, hearing their excited voices as they looked up towards the stratosphere, then he felt a wave of heat on his cheek like the sun coming from behind a cloud on a cold morning. It grew warmer, and Cheiron forced his gaze around. To his horror, he saw thin trails of smoke emerging at various points from the stratosphere. He craned his neck upwards and noticed that the stratosphere was glowing dim orange around the laser reflector on top of the craft. *The reflector must've been damaged by the storm!* Cheiron thought. *The orbiter's laser is being absorbed by the 'sphere!* He ran towards the stratosphere, jumping from the rocks. 'Stop receiving! Tell the orbiter to stop trans . . .'

The stratosphere began to change colour from bright red, through orange to white . . . The entycraft exploded suddenly and without warning Cheiron was knocked over by the force of the explosion. In the same instant he realised with a sick feeling that by now the Doctor, Captain and Centurion were probably burnt to cinders on the flight deck. He went cold at the thought of them sitting there, a wave of searing heat slashing through their bodies . . . Then the stratosphere pulsated twice. It was now just a white, throbbing ball of intense heat. Cheiron scrambled to his feet and had the impulse to try to get his crew out of the inferno . . . remembered that they could not have survived . . . started back . . .

The blast took hold of his body and threw him, flailing helplessly, over the edge of the sheer drop. The sky spun over his head twice, three times and he sensed the ground come up to slam hard against his back as he saw billowing black clouds pour over the edge along with long tails of orange flame. His head bounced on impact and his senses reeled. The world toppling around him, he tried to get up and look around to see what had happened, where he was, and then a silver wave splashed over his mind, and turned to red . . .

The Cloudspeople

For a lifetime, Cheiron lay looking blankly into the sky down a long, orange tube. Then life began again. There was some shuffling about and his senses began to return to him. He moved his head to the side and the sky moved upwards. His eyes ached from the change in the intensity of the light. He felt cold, damp sand in his hair and ears. There were feet as well. Numerous pairs of feet, mostly bare with writhing toes as the sand cut in between them, but there were some with sandals on and one pair that peered from beneath a robe, clad in leather.

Hands. Hands took hold of him under the armpits and he felt the heaviness of blood rushing out of his head and nose. He could feel the pulse in his temples and hear his heart beating in his ears. His head flopped on to his chest and the sand fell from his hair on to his shirt. His back felt cold from the ground. Saliva dribbled from his mouth. A dull ache came and went and came again in his left arm. Soon it stung, and he felt warm blood on his skin as the people with hands and feet carried him away from the ridge on which he had landed. Those feet scuffled on the sandstone that had soaked up the water and was drying to a dull grey colour. They hauled him up the rocks and then he felt grass through his boots. The smell of vegetation mingled with the smell of burning. He raised his head and opened his eyes fully. They had halted and looked at the pile of blackened, tangled metal which smouldered before them. He looked up and saw long, curving ribs charred and broken reaching into the overcast sky. Cheiron tried to scream, groaned and they turned away.

They went to the village on the hill, surrounded and obscured by hedges and trees. It consisted of a cluster of huts of various shapes and sizes, all constructed in a crude fashion from grasses and rushes and branches from trees.

They carried Cheiron, stumbling over the slippery ground, to the largest of the huts. Through the dizzy mist that shrouded his tormented consciousness, Cheiron made out the building's long, rectangular shape and noticed that it had been constructed with a great deal more care than the other huts.

They passed through the heavy, wet curtain that served as a door and carried Cheiron to a pile of furs on the rush matting near the brazier that smoked and crackled with dim and distant ashes which must have been burning for a long time. There they laid him down and built up the fire.

A young woman with short, wavy blonde hair tended his wounds with strange medicinal herbs and Cheiron fell asleep whilst her soft hands stroked his brow and sapped the conscious thoughts from his mind, drawing out the energy from his limbs. He lapsed into a sleep of angry dreams and bizarre images.

Cheiron woke in the early hours of the morning. He felt certain that the whole thing had been a nightmare . . . he found it so difficult to make definite recollections of what had transpired. And yet, when he gripped his bed with his hand, he found it to be soft fur. He opened his eyes. Grim daylight filtered in from behind the curtain in the doorway. There were the sounds of strange people sleeping around him. He shifted his aching neck and saw men wrapped in their furs, snoring and chewing over their dreams. He was suddenly reminded of the Aoidni. Primitive.

After a long time in the twilight of sleep, the village began to awaken. Cheiron tried to get up from the rugs on which he lay, but found that he could hardly move his left arm. Any attempt at movement was very painful.

The woman who had tended his wounds the night before came to him again. She had blue eyes and a shrew-like face. The eyes seemed too small for the rest of her face, and they were penetrating, like those of untamed mice.

'How do you feel?' the woman asked in a slightly cracked voice, yet full of life and emotion.

Cheiron was surprised that she was able to speak the Imperial tongue. He remembered the man in the leather shoes . . . 'I ache all over . . .'

'You didn't break any bones. You'll live.' She smiled softly with pinkish lips.

'My arm . . .'

'Just a slight cut . . . well, a large cut, but it'll heal if you give it chance. I'll put a fresh dressing on it for you.'

She took hold of his arm and began removing a long strip of cloth that had been wound around his arm over the wound. Cheiron noticed how surprisingly soft her touch was. Her skin had the feel of perfect gentleness, like the skin of a child a few months after birth.

'What is this place?' Cheiron asked her as she put the bandage aside.

'The hill is called Stoney Clouds. The Teller will come and speak with you soon. He will tell you all that you wish to know.'

'Teller? There's a Teller here?' The man with leather shoes, Cheiron thought.

'There is always a Teller here. What is your name?'

'Cheiron. Cheiron Androcles.' He was uninterested in names at this moment. He had to speak to the Teller quickly.

'My name is Ylain.'

Ylain? Ylain? That's surely not an Imperial name. How strange. I've never encountered names within the Empire which bear no relation to the Imperial names, he thought abstractedly. 'What does Ylain mean?'

'Ylain means "fawn".' She expertly wrapped a new bandage around the wound and secured it tightly. 'There. It is done. It will not take very long to heal.'

'When will the Teller come?' Cheiron wanted to know.

Ylain stood up. 'He has first to tell the people their horoscopes, then he will come and talk with you I think. I shall tell him that you wish to speak with him.'

'Thank you.' Cheiron relaxed as Ylain left the hut.

Before the Teller came, Cheiron lay deep in thought about

the three men who had been killed in the explosion. Through memories that aroused angry sorrow, his thoughts wandered to ways in which the accident could have been avoided, and then bizarre hope crept up on him and intensified the sorrow when it saw reality and fled.

Cheiron's eyes were shut when the Teller came into the hut. He blinked them open when he heard the soft footsteps padding over the rushes.

'I am sorry that I was delayed, but there are many things I have to attend to each day,' the old, bald Teller explained. His voice was gentle, yet somehow firm. It was a smiling, ironic voice and full of wisdom. It was a real Teller's voice.

This is a clever one. I've little reason to be at all dishonest in his presence, Cheiron thought. 'No need to apologise. What is your name? I am Cheiron Androcles, a Senator of the Imperial government. Not that it matters now.'

The old man sat down on the floor next to Cheiron and supported himself with one hand. 'I am called Theobule by the people of the Imperium, but I am also called Alvis by the Cloudspeople.'

'Cloudspeople?'

'The hill on which this village stands is called Stoney Clouds. The people who live here are called the Cloudspeople. There are other peoples in the valley, too, such as the inhabitants of Stoney Village, the Hermits who dwell in the wood which closes on one side of the land of the Brotherhood and the Dalesmen.'

'I've a lot to discover for myself when I am well.'

'What destroyed your stratosphere?'

'We had to ride a storm coming down. We had it pretty rough. When we had landed, an orbiter tried to make contact using lasers. Our reflector must've been damaged. The orbiter's laser sliced into the stratosphere, then overheated the craft . . . must've been quite a few thousand degrees . . . then that was it. My three crewmen were killed. They must have been burnt to nothing within seconds of the laser penetrating the hull . . .'

'I'm sorry about your friends, Senator. Let us be thankful that you are alive. Why have you come here?'

Cheiron laboriously explained about the space warp and the Duke's idea for getting to the Great Belt.

'That is interesting,' the Teller said. There was a hint of

smugness in his voice that made Cheiron feel ill at ease. 'Are you sure that you have left nothing out?'

'I have personal reasons for coming here also. Reasons to do with the Tellers, and the Lords of the Zodiac, and a certain "Devil god" which I know very little about, I'm afraid.' I wonder how he'll react to that last statement.

'Really. I can see that there is destiny in your hands, Cheiron Androcles. I can more than feel it within you.'

'I have been told that before by wise men. I also have much blood on my hands. Do you resent the destiny being put into the hands of one such as I?'

'How can I resent the divine course I follow, which we all follow, but ones such as myself more particularly? I know that there is blood and great sorrow on your hands. I feel that something has started on Acima . . . in the Dale. You must concentrate on getting well. Let your mind be flexible towards the heavens. You may well have been chosen to perform some great task. You must let the Lords of the Zodiac come into your soul and replenish its spiritual strength.'

'I feel so helpless lying here . . . '

'You are not one who likes to be out of action for too long,' the Teller stood up and smoothed his gown. 'Tomorrow, you may get up. We will arrange a feast and make merry. There will be times when you will need sweet memories to give you heart. Do not be afraid of the awesome destiny which engulfs you.' With that, the Teller walked slowly from the hut. The curtain fell behind him and Cheiron felt suddenly sad, angry and excited all at once. He tried in vain to sleep the day away.

Stoney Clouds

The next morning, Cheiron walked with the Teller Alvis away from the village of the Cloudspeople. They walked steadily towards the horizon, formed by the hill, to the west, and talked.

'How did you come to Stoney Clouds?' Cheiron asked the Teller.

'I am a native of Acima.'

Cheiron seemed surprised.

'I was educated in the Imperium after being taken from my home on Stoney Clouds by a Teller who came here in a small spaceship when I was very young. I was taught all there is to know about the Second Empire of New Earth – more than even you as a Senator will know. I was also trained in the ways of the Tellers and certain of the Laws and history of the Zodiac.'

They had reached the top of the hill. Here, Stoney Clouds ended by slowly melting into a forest. Two tracks led from Stoney Clouds into it. Alvis did not move when they had reached the apex of the hill, and Cheiron halted also. It was a drizzly morning, and a fine spray of water blew from the east. Dark clouds clung to the sky and blended with each other to produce a dark and watery panorama.

'When did you return here?' Cheiron queried.

'I returned ten Standard Years ago, under orders from the High Table of Bards and Tellers. Acima has a lot to do with the destiny of the omniverse, though more particularly with the galaxy for the next few aeons, or so I understand.' He spoke with amusement in his tone. People usually would scorn that remark.

Cheiron did not scorn. He thought: Destiny. Everywhere I go I hear talk of destiny, fate and Tellers. What does it all mean? Am I any nearer to the end of this quest across the galaxy? Is it all a futile chase after nothing? . . . No, there has to be something behind all this. Something which connects Acima, the Tellers, the Devil-god and the Lords of the Zodiac and *me*, and destiny . . . Cheiron nervously put his hand inside the shirt he had been given and pulled out the pendant with its picture of the Devil-god. He had worn it ever since he had acquired it. He undid the catch on the chain and handed it to Alvis. 'What do you make of this? It shows the Devil-god that I spoke of earlier.'

'The Thirteenth Sign,' Alvis said, letting the light run over the features of the picture. 'Just as Capricorn is the goat, and Pisces is the fish, Satan is the devil. Where did you get this?'

'I took it from a man who tried to kill me. Is it significant?'

'The pieces of a puzzle which you presented me with now begin to fall into place. Who is your Lord?'

'Lord Aries governs the steps I follow. Can you tell me more of the great destiny I have yet to follow?'

'A little, perhaps.' Alvis's leather-clad feet squished in the wet grass.

'Then tell me what this "Satan" Lord is.'

Alvis sighed. 'Satan the devil is a renegade Lord of the Zodiac. He is the twin brother of Lady Gemini, whom we call the "twins", though in fact the Gemini twins constitute two signs of the Zodiac. Satan's aim is to dominate. He prefers to rule alone, rather than be bound by the Lords of the Zodiac who each "control" only one part in thirteen. Satan wishes to dominate all. I cannot tell you why, because I don't know.'

'Does he dwell apart from the other Lords?'

'We do not know where our Lords dwell, but we can be sure that Lord Satan dwells separately from the others. Among the twelve signs there is sympathy for Satan's mysterious aims coming from the direction of Taurus. But I can only glean small facts from legends and put them into a factual account for your ears. There is little else to tell.'

Cheiron took the pendant back from Alvis and secured it around his own neck. He looked into the Teller's face, which dripped water from aged features, moulded into a lean face, and bald head where purple veins pulsed. 'Will you ask for guidance from Lord Aries for me?'

'Of course. I am under strict orders to follow any line of fate which has a connection with the fate of Acima.'

'I must warn you, Alvis, that the last Teller who read me a personal horoscope died before he could give it to me. Satan's followers, I suppose.'

'I have little to fear from the followers of Lord Satan. They are few and far between. Satan has to rely on converts from other signs' followers to constitute the bulk of his own. There are no followers of Satan on Stoney Clouds. They exist only in Izembard.'

'Izembard?'

Alvis turned and indicated the industrial complex with a wave of his arm through the saturated air. 'Izembard,' he repeated. 'A place completely dominated by the laws of Satan. There are many things going on beneath that curtain of pollution and grime. Many things. There, Satan works his plans on mortals. There are occasional raids into the Dale from Izembard, but they enjoy little success. There have been no raids for a few years now. I don't know whether that is good or bad.'

'There are people in that mess?'

'If you choose to call them that. They are not people like you and I. They are adapted to exist in that place. To breathe the atmosphere of Izembard would mean death to us after a while. Once, the people there were like us. Once they farmed the land and raised cattle like us . . . now they are the puppets of the Countess of Izembard. They feed on their own dead and spend their lives toiling over Satan's experiments for later use on the whole of humankind.' Alvis's face contorted in disgust as he recited the grim details.

'Who is this Countess? Is she an Imperial Countess?'

'No. She is some obscure woman from a long, long dead age. I have heard tell that she originated in the dark past of New Earth, before the Apocalypse, before New Earth was NEW Earth. I know so very little of these things. The raiders she sends always try to steal maidens from the Dale. There is a theory that they use these to reproduce their vile species. Or perhaps the Countess uses them for a special purpose . . . '

Surely this is evil? And yet I was warned not to think in terms of good and evil. I am to choose between the twelve signs of the Zodiac and the Thirteenth? How can I choose if I don't even know this Lord Satan's motivations? 'Has Izembard ever been penetrated?'

'It would be beyond the wildest dreams of these people even to try. Besides, it is impossible to leave the Dale.'

'How is it impossible?'

'You can follow the tracks leading out of the Dale, but they always lead you back. You can leave the tracks and go your own way using any kind of navigational device you care to mention, but you will always end up back in the Dale. The only way to get out is to fly out. These people did not inherit space travel from their ancestors as did the men of New Earth.'

'Then I have a problem if I am to follow this trail to its end. Perhaps Lord Aries will show me the way. Who are the rulers of the Dale?'

'Ah! Our blessed rulers! The mighty overlords!' Alvis said with sarcasm. 'We are ruled by a group of petty tyrants known as the Brotherhood. They live in a great building surrounded by their lands and those of the Dalesmen, who are the wealthiest and most fortunate inhabitants of the Dale. The Brotherhood scorn the Zodiac. They worship a religion of which they know only a little, handed down from the dim past. They have a great book which no one can read and which they claim to follow. The High Table of Bards and Tellers have found it to be entitled "The Holy Bible". What they claim to be presented as "truths" in this book are, in fact, only their guesses as to what it contains. The result of this is viciousness and tyranny. For many days in the lives of the people, we have to work their lands and tend their cattle while the Brotherhood go about imposing their strict rulings on us.' There was hate in his tone now.

Xenophon spoke of this, Cheiron recalled. This strange book which the Tellers read and scorn the simplicity of and which has been wrongly translated by this Brotherhood, resulting in the hate communicated in this native's voice. Yet this is a step nearer to the Divine. Perhaps the Brotherhood can give me a clue to my journey's end. Cheiron looked out to the black expanse of Izembard, towering in grim magnificence through the filth which shrouded it. I feel sure that I have to go to Izembard. Only then can I discover what the ideas of Satan the Devil are, and whether they are right for the requirements of mankind. I may even find out how the choice is to be made . . . 'Shall we go back to the village, Alvis?'

'If you have no more questions. I do not like discussing such things in the presence of the Cloudspeople. It puts fear into their simple minds when others speak of involved doctrine.'

'I have no more questions for now. When I have talked to the Cloudspeople, and feel that I know them, I'll go to the wreck of the stratosphere and mourn my friends.'

'A worthy gesture, Cheiron Androcles. I envy you not the burden you carry on your shoulders. Mourn in peace. Peace is what you will need.'

The two men set off over the lush grass towards the village with its noises and woodsmoke, and Cheiron listened to the birdcalls in the rainy morning breeze.

Gael

While the flames leaped from the fire, and the Cloudspeople sang their merry ballads, Cheiron Androcles turned over in his mind the things that the Teller Alvis had told him that morning. He sat near to the fire through no choosing of his own and watched the flames lick the dark sky. Occasionally, he sipped a bitter drink from a wooden bowl and licked it from his lips.

I cannot leave the Dale . . . and yet the raiders from Izembard seem to be able to get in and out . . . perhaps if I were to be captured in their next raid . . . but I'm not a pretty maiden. What will Duke Dolophious be doing now? His thoughts were interrupted.

'I am Gael,' a female voice said. 'What is your name? I knew what it was, but it is a very difficult name and I've forgotten it.'

'Er – sorry . . . You were saying . . . ?'

'What is your *name*?'

Cheiron looked up into a smooth, white face with brown eyes which reflected the intensity of the fire, and hair the texture of wool that hung about a face in profusion. In the light of the fire, against the dark background, it shone like the colour of platinum. 'I am Cheiron Androcles.'

The full red lips parted into a half-smile, revealing teeth of brilliant white. 'That is a funny name. What does your name mean?'

'My name means something like "the hand of the glory of men". It is a strange meaning. My name is very old. I don't fully understand it.'

Gael smiled again and tilted her head to one side. She sat down beside him and placed her hands on her knees. She craned forwards and turned her head to look into Cheiron's face. He drank from the bowl of ale and grimaced as she watched him drink.

'Would you like to know what my name means?' Gael asked. She sat upright, as did he.

Cheiron was feeling happier. One day of mourning is enough for any man's soul in such a place as this. I shall be merry! 'If you would like to tell me the meaning of your name.'

'Gael means "merry",' Gael answered. She seemed proud of her name. She seemed a proud woman.

Coincidence, he wondered? I shall indeed be merry!

The Cloudspeople danced around their fire and supped their bitter ale and laughed and sang jovially. Gael and Cheiron danced around the fire too, simply and delightfully whirling as the drink took effect. At first, Cheiron was embarrassed, but eventually he learned that these people lacked all of the sophistications of the Empire and the dance was simple . . . whirl!

Gael's mother was a fat, laughing lady with shabby, grey-brown hair. She watched them, clapped, sung and became slowly drunker and drunker until she slumped into her man's lap.

The next morning they took three horses, which Gael reported were the pride of the Cloudspeople, and Cheiron, Gael and her friend Ylain rode off in the direction of Stoney Village. The morning was warm, and the clouded sky interlaced by a washed-out blue. The sun that Duke Dolophious had called Phi-Omega shone brightly through the clear space of sky and gave the land an overall summery appearance. As they rode, Cheiron smelled the odour of the grass and the trees and the wild flowers, and he found it exceedingly pleasant. It had been a long time since he had had the pleasure of riding gently through green pastures in warm sunshine with the fresh smell of the summertime round about.

The horses were nimble creatures, and were the colour of sand in the evening as the sun set over the arid Lands of the Aoidni. And when Cheiron contemplated this, he felt homesick despite the pleasantness of the world around him.

They rose slowly over the flat land of lush grass, and then on to a road that wound uphill through the trees which cast their shadows on to its rough surface. The road took them into Stoney Village. The village was a collection of a few rough streets without any kind of surfacing. The cottages were superior to the huts of the Cloudspeople, though they had seemed the same from the air owing to their clumsily thatched roofs.

'Shall we call at the alehouse?' Gael asked Ylain and Cheiron.

'I could drink the river dry!' Ylain answered.

'I hope they don't make the ale with the water of the river!' Cheiron exclaimed.

Gael led the way along the short streets. The village's inhabitants were nowhere to be seen, only a few scruffy children and an old man walking slowly along with the aid of a crooked stick. He watched the three riders pass and grinned with a toothless mouth and waved in a friendly manner with his stick. Gael ignored the gesture, but Ylain smiled an enchanting smile and bade the old man good day.

'Where are all the people?' Cheiron asked.

'They'll be at work,' Gael answered. 'Some of them will be

at their own farms and some on the lands of the Brotherhood.'

The alehouse was a squat, brown building with wild roses creeping up its wooden walls, so that it was immersed in lush blooms and greenery.

They dismounted and tied the three ponies up outside the alehouse on fences specially erected for that purpose. They entered the tavern through a low doorway constructed of heavy beams with cracked and aged carvings on them. Inside, there was an overpowering smell of age and ale. The alehouse was empty but for the landlord and a pair of old men who occupied a corner of the room near a dusty window. Scattered around the floor were rough benches. The only table in the room was enormous, of carved wood, behind which the fat landlord stood and behind him were several barrels standing on end with tankards clustered around them on the stone floor. Silver insects hummed and danced in the air.

Ylain and Cheiron went to one of the benches and sat down while Gael went to buy three bowls of the landlord's best ale.

Ylain bent towards Cheiron and asked quietly: 'Do you like Gael?'

Cheiron glanced at Gael who was waiting at the table for the landlord to measure out the drink from one of the barrels.

'Very much,' Cheiron replied, and he couldn't resist a smile of embarrassment.

'Where is your home, Cheiron? What are the women there like?'

'Alvis must've told you something about the stars that you can see at night and the people who come out of the sky from them . . . '

'He has told us a little.'

'I came here out of the sky, from one of those stars. You cannot see my star from here, but it is there in the space beyond the sky.'

Gael brought the drinks and sat down.

'And the women on your star?' Ylain persisted.

'Oh, they are not very nice women. For the most part they are whores. In the great city of New Incarnation they are grander – courtesans.'

They drank together.

'What would you like to do when we have finished here?' Gael asked Cheiron.

'It's up to you, I'm your guest,' Cheiron said.

'I think I will return,' Ylain said, hurriedly finishing her drink.

'We will see you later,' Gael said as Ylain stood up.

'Don't hurry,' Ylain smiled, and left the inn. Shortly afterwards, they heard the sound of hooves going off down the road.

Cheiron finished his ale, and Gael followed suit. 'Where to now?' he asked her.

'We can ride up to the lands of the Brotherhood, if you so wish, provided that we don't attract too much attention.'

They are so afraid of this Brotherhood. It seems incredible that they should have such a fear for mere primitives when they sit on the very doorstep of the Confederacy of Planets. But then these people are also primitive. 'That will be most interesting.'

They reached their destination shortly after midday. It was a distance of about seven kilometres to the lands of the Brotherhood. As they rode down the last steep hill, Cheiron saw the strange, large building once more in the middle distance. 'What is that place?' he asked, indicating the construction. Figures moved around it.

'The Great House of the Brotherhood. That is their home. It is the most magnificent building in all of the Dale. There are bigger things in Izembard, but that is not in the Dale, and besides, Izembard is a filthy place.'

They came smoothly to a halt and looked out over the rolling land to the Great House. It was surrounded by a low wall and beyond that were patchwork fields of variously coloured crops, but the accent seemed to be on cattle, which roamed freely on large expanses of rough pasture. The scene was flanked on the left by a wood of tall trees which covered an embankment. The trees made a boundary as they spilled over the hill towards the lands of the Brotherhood and the village which was gathered about a single, long road which was the shape of the hind leg of a hound.

Gael noticed Cheiron's eyes scrutinising the trees with their luxuriant foliage. 'That is the Hermit's Wood,' she told him. 'It is inhabited by numerous outlaws. Once, there was only one hermit who fled from the Great House. That was a long time ago, but they say that he still lives with the outlaws! He must be too old to move!'

'Perhaps it's just a story,' Cheiron suggested. 'Do we go any further?'

'I think not. The Brotherhood and their home unnerve me. May we go back?'

'You're the guide. I'll follow.'

Gael wheeled her horse and started back up the hill. Cheiron followed her, watching the little horse's head move up and down as it panted and struggled in the heat. He urged his horse to Gael's side.

'Where I come from, the horse is a great and mighty beast. We use the horse as a weapon of war,' Cheiron explained.

'There have been no wars here for a long time. These are the best mounts that the Dale can produce.'

'Tell me more about your history.'

'Where would you like me to begin?'

'At the beginning.'

'There are many stories. The story that Alvis tells us that is nearest to the truth is the one about the eggs.'

'Eggs . . . ?'

'Yes. It is said that once a great bird came here and it laid great silver eggs. Some say there were three, some say there were two. But from these eggs hatched the first men of the Dale. The great bird had journeyed far to come here and had been sent by the God of the Brotherhood. The first people multiplied and began to cultivate the land and the animals which they found living here they domesticated and with their mighty power they changed some of the animals into new animals so that they were better. But after a long time, the first people died and left their daughters and sons, and they died and left theirs. The great bird never returned to take anyone home. After many generations, they forgot many of the words of their forefathers and they destroyed the great and mighty power by smashing the shells of the silver eggs and using them to make weapons and houses and trinkets. After more generations, they built the Great House and the people degenerated from their divine ancestors. Some of the people went to Izembard and built that place where once there were green fields. These, we are told, were cleverer than the people in the Dale.

'But the eggs had been laid on other parts of our world, far away. These were evil eggs of an ugly bird and they were the colour of blood. And it was said that their mother the great red bird was spawned of the red star that does not burn in the heavens but in the depths of hell. And in the homeland of the people of the Dale there was a war waged with great fury between the followers of the bird of the silver eggs and that spawned of the great red star. And the people of the red eggs on this world wished to continue the war here. And our world was thrown into war also. There was great destruction, and allies and enemies sprung from everywhere. Great fire and smoke fell from the skies and the green fields turned to black desert. Then, after the war, only the Dale and Izembard were left, for the people of the Dale were saved by their ignorance of the super-weapons of their ancestors. There followed a plague of horrible sickness, and many died. Then, those who were left multiplied again and again and were twice smitten by the plague until it went away. Then there was left only those who had fled to the Great House for the sanctuary of their God, whose name and teachings they had forgotten long since. And so they worshipped blindly. And then some of the people ventured out into the Dale and began to farm and live again, whilst always giving thanks to their God for deliverance from the Holocaust, for that is the name given to the war and the plague. The Great House became the place of ruling of the Dale and was kept by the Holy Order of the Brotherhood who began to rediscover the teachings of their God.'

They turned the corner on to a road that led to Stoney Village. The road which they had left went on uphill, and Cheiron wondered where it led to. Then he turned his interest back to Gael's recital of the legends. 'Please continue, Gael.'

'Well, many ages passed and the long seasons of our world came and went. During this time, the Brotherhood rose to the heights of tyranny (that isn't in the "official" version of the legend), and the people of Izembard were happiest because they did not fear the Brotherhood. Then there was a change. Izembard began to grow, for some strange and wicked magic was working within it. It is said that Izembard was being punished for disobedience by the God of the Brotherhood. There was blackness and destructive smoke in Izembard, and the river which had delighted the people of the Dale for generations ran red with the life-blood of the creatures which lived within. The river soon became void of all life. The people thirsted and the land was parched, for the rain was also polluted by the evil of Izembard. Then, one of the Brotherhood's number was walking on their lands one day when he had a wonderful vision. He saw twelve great lights in the sky, and each light took a form and beckoned him towards the wooded slopes. And in a place where once there had been trees, but had been cleared by the Brotherhood, the grass became wet beneath his feet. The sky darkened and it thundered and rain began to pour and pour. Then the lights vanished. Each day, brother Michael went to the land where he had been led and each day the ground became wetter and wetter until at last the water burst through the soil. And suddenly, the rain was clean again and the Dale thrived. Brother Michael went away from the Great House, denouncing the falseness of the God they had worshipped, and became a hermit in the wood, for he was led there by a silvery orb that appeared in the sky and hung over the wood for a night. And there, as I have told you, he is still supposed to dwell. After that, outlaws from all over the Dale fled to the Hermit's Wood and now the Brotherhood cannot go too close to the trees lest they do not return.

'Then the Tellers came from the great beyond and influenced us greatly, because they too arrived in silver eggs and said that they had been brought by the great space-bird. The Tellers taught us many things, even the language which you and I speak. The Brotherhood denounced the Tellers, but had to adopt their language after a while so as to make themselves understood in the Dale. Meanwhile, Izembard became more and more dangerous and there were raids. The raids took place when a great mist rolled over the hills and into the Dale and the creatures of Izembard came and stole all the virgins they could find and proclaimed that they were doing the bidding of the Countess who was the ruler of Izembard. You know the rest of our history.'

Cheiron was thoughtful. There were so many points in the legends which fitted into rational explanations. 'Thank you, Gael. I am beginning to see things as they really are, now.' Now he realised more than ever that there was little to be learned in the Dale, the people were too simple. I have to get to Izembard and find out what it is that motivates the place to fester in all of that pollution. Who is this countess? Why do they only steal virgins? If they want to reproduce they would not *have* to have virginal breeding stock, surely, he pondered.

The road to Stoney Village was long, and for Gael it was uncomfortable in the heat of the day. For Cheiron, it was another reminder of what it was like in the Lands of the Aoidni, but for the grass that grew abundantly in the Dale, the smaller horses and the lower temperature.

They arrived back at Stoney Clouds in the late afternoon,

and Cheiron saw first of all the ribs of the stratosphere reaching skywards like the bones of some long dead behemoth, charred and blackened. Sadness began to well up from its source in his stomach, to his heart and his mind. But he told himself of the deaths he had witnessed before, the lives he had taken. The sadness abated somewhat.

In the evening, when memories of the day swam serenely through his mind, Cheiron walked with Gael through the woods on Stoney Clouds after scrambling on the sandstone outcroppings to get to the sparse stand of small trees which played like children on the uneven topography. She wore a long, flowing gown which was decorated delicately and hugged her figure sensitively in the fading light. They sat down for a while on a fallen log at the foot of an outcropping and didn't speak. Cheiron felt as though he wanted to hold her and kiss her and make love to her beneath the starry blanket of the night, but she remained somehow aloof and looked as though to have touched her would be indecent and he didn't want to offend her dignity. He watched her profile and then she turned to him. 'When will you be leaving to follow this quest of yours that everyone talks about? You are something of an enigma in the village . . .'

'Oh, I don't know. I have to get to Izembard, I think, and I'm told that that's impossible. I'll have to wait until I can find a way. Besides, I have no wish to leave . . . now . . .'

'Why not?'

'Because . . . because of you . . .'

'Why me?'

'Why does any man want to remain close to a woman . . . ?'

'Any woman?'

'All right then, *his* woman!'

'I'm not your woman, yet.'

'Would you like to be?'

'I might . . . yes. Yes, I think that I would. But you must never leave me.'

He knew that such a promise was impossible to fulfil, yet he found himself saying, 'I'll never leave you.'

Gael stood up and smothed her gown. 'You will not touch me until our wedding night, you understand. You may hold my hand only, according to my family custom . . .'

Cheiron stood up. 'V-very well.'

Gael walked away, back towards the track leading through

the trees, she ran her fingers through her flowing hair and seemed happy in a strange way. Cheiron looked back at the log on which they had sat. The towering rocks leered at him, and he felt inferior. He followed Gael into the trees.

Ylain

Although her parents (particularly her mother) were delighted with the news of her engagement to the distinguished stranger, Gael herself seemed indifferent. Cheiron was depressed by her manner, but he had convinced himself that he loved Gael, had been caught up by some alien emotion, even though he realised that they could never truly share a genuine relationship.

It was a few days after their agreement that the Clouds-people left their village in the pouring rain on their way to work the lands of the Brotherhood. Only a few remained to tend the animals and to look after their visitor's needs. Gael was among those who stayed behind, along with Alvis.

The rain had relented slightly by the time that Cheiron and Alvis, watching from one of the outcroppings known as Dead Man's Rock, saw the stream of people disappear into the trees in the direction of Stoney Village.

When only the birds, the rain and the distant groanings of Izembard could be heard, Alvis turned to Cheiron and said: 'So, you're to be married.'

'Yes . . . yes I am. To Gael.'

Alvis nodded. 'You're sure that you want to marry her?'

'Yes, absolutely.'

'Lord Aries is not so sure, Cheiron Androcles.'

'What do you mean? You've read the stars?'

The water ran down Alvis's features and made his bald head glisten. 'I have. You are warned to beware of love at present. A woman could bring about your fall from your duty. A woman might cause you to fail in your task, especially if that woman is Gael.'

'*No!* I will not listen! Lord Aries did not say that!'

'The stars do not specify, of course – '

'Well then.'

' – But I know Gael. Gael is ambitious and proud above all else. She would like to marry you and keep you around to demonstrate her influence over you. Gael – the great defier of destiny, thwarter of the great Lords! Don't you see, Cheiron? These people are capable of greed and pride and jealousy the same as any others.'

'And *love*.'

Alvis smiled. For a moment there was silence, and rain, then: 'Love,' he said softly. 'You have come here, across the Empire from the rat-race of New Earth. You have known only war and sorrow and death, hatred and strife, so you try to extract joy and life and love from the first woman you meet who isn't from a sexual selection company. You are so vulnerable on the inside, Cheiron, beneath all that confidence you have in yourself. Wait, imprison your heart and put your soul into the task at hand.'

Cheiron heard footsteps and turned and looked up at the grassy slope behind the outcropping. Gael stood poised on the edge of the sandy dip that led down to the rock. Her jaw stiffened and there was a grim and brooding anger in her eyes, but no sorrow at the words she had overheard. Cheiron was lost for words, taken by surprise.

'You will be no loss to me,' Gael said. 'You can go off on your ridiculous quest and I hope that you don't get back alive!' and with that she turned with a toss of her hair and walked back towards the village proudly erect, with her finely-shaped hips swaggering beneath the short brown skirt.

Cheiron thought of running after her. He looked around at Alvis and saw an uninterested smile on his lips. 'Now see what you've done!'

'Control your desperate feelings; suppress them. Look deep inside yourself and you'll see what I mean. Look at that jelly-like mass that was once a warrior, a warlord who defied the might of an empire at its heart. What do you think, Cheiron Androcles? Do you see the man you used to be before you came here?'

Damn him! He's right. Why did I fall for Gael the way I did? Was it what he said about the rat-race? I said the same thing when I told Ylain about the whores on New Earth. 'No, no I don't see the man who led the Aoidni in battle against the Imperial forces or those of the governors of the districts in those lands. You're right Alvis. I've developed an apathy lately.'

'You must not lose your sense of purpose. You must fight to regain your character.'

'Yes, yes I must. Did Lord Aries give me any further guidance?'

'I feel that soon there will be something of a catastrophe. Lord Aries warns you that you will face a great trial at the hands of an unknown enemy. Not a safe outlook, but don't forget that it's only a projection of the future, and you could avert it if you tried hard enough.'

'I'll take the trial, I think. I'm content to be guided by Lord Aries for the time being until the time comes when I reach the end of this quest, for better or for worse.'

The Cloudspeople returned to their homes after a day and a half of working on the lands of the Brotherhood. In accordance with their festive nature, they set about building a fire for dancing and drinking on the night of their return. Cheiron was glad to help them, but avoided contact with Gael, who sauntered around the village going about her menial tasks with characteristic reluctance and misplaced dignity.

When the fire was lit and the grass began to steam with the heat of the blaze, Cheiron retreated to the back of the crowd of people and talked at length to Alvis about his experiences in the Empire and on the planet Acima.

After some time, Cheiron slowly overcame the disquiet in his mind about what had happened with Gael and joined in with the intoxicating whirling dance of the Cloudspeople as they sang their fast songs which contained little hint of sadness.

As the night drew on, a boy with a small stringed instrument was at last urged to play a tune for the people. As the boy took up his position on the other side of the dying fire, a group of women flocked over to Cheiron and asked him if he would take this dance in the company of Ylain, Gael's friend. They explained that the dance was slow involving a simple side-to-side movement while in a not-too-intimate embrace. Cheiron agreed and the boy began to play. Other couples joined in the dance, and the music was beautiful. Cheiron slipped his hands gently around Ylain's waist and followed her movements. She seemed to be trembling slightly, almost imperceptibly and seemed for some reason unable to look him directly in the eye.

When the dance was over, Cheiron released Ylain and thanked her and returned to his position in the crowd as the more typical dancing began again. Cheiron was quick to involve himself in it all and began singing along with the rest of them.

As the couples began to depart to their beds, and the children began to fall asleep where they sat, Cheiron walked away from the fire and felt the cool breeze on his face. He stretched himself and felt somehow at peace with the omniverse that night. He walked a little further, clearing the woodsmoke from his lungs, and then he heard the sound of someone crying. He halted and his ears directed his eyes towards a clump of black bushes. He listened to the sobbing, and the voice from which it was derived saying words which he could not hear properly. He knew the voice as Ylain's. There were other voices too, female. He walked in the direction of the bushes and one of the other women saw him from behind the leaves. She ran towards him. He stopped and a tall, fair woman looked at him embarrassedly.

'What's happening?' Cheiron asked, nodding in the direction of the bushes.

'It's Ylain. She is crying – for, for you. I think that Ylain has a great affection for you . . . '

'Ask her to come to me.'

The woman nodded. 'Ylain! Come out!'

Ylain emerged after a little coaxing, along with her friends. Cheiron advanced towards her and stretched out his hand. He felt her soft hand gently rest in his palm and his fingers closed unsurely over hers. They walked slowly away until they could see beyond the bushes that grew in profusion here, to the lights of Izembard. They halted there and stood alone on the hillside as though they owned the night, as though the stars were simply there to watch over the two of them, as though no one else existed or had the right to exist. Cheiron turned to face her. She was a little shorter than himself with fine, wavy blonde hair which was held in place by a broad and elaborate hair-decoration. Tears streaked her delicate features and Cheiron wiped her cheeks with his finger. 'Don't cry, Ylain,' he said in a low voice.

'I'm sorry,' she sobbed.

'Don't be sorry.' His arms folded around her waist and he tilted his head to bring his lips down to her lovely mouth.

They made love in the dew, and when it was over they put on their soaking garments and walked hand-in-hand back to the fire which dwindled in the middle distance.

There had been another time. Her name was Semele. Her

home was in New Incarnation, that city of the spires like slender daggers, twinkling in the light of the sun, moon and stars, poised to strike into the heart of the universe. He had seen her on a bright, windswept day so typical of the summers in the northern regions of New Earth. It had been many years ago, almost an eternity. He had walked through the old quarter of the capital with its huddled streets and old houses that reached out to each other so that sometimes the sky could hardly be seen between them. A student at the university of New Incarnation, Cheiron Androcles was a mere eighteen summers of age and very naïve. He was tall and slender with short black hair and long, sinewy arms under one of which he clutched some of his books so that they stabbed into his ribs and he'd know if he dropped one of them on his journey back to his lodgings at noon.

Semele he had seen looking out of one of those high windows in the old wooden houses. She hung out of the window with her eyes looking skywards and her long blonde hair curling gently in the breeze. Semele was a little older than himself and was uneducated, and knew the ways of the world well enough to be able to attract the attentions of a young man who took her fancy, who seemed to delight in walking along the streets of New Incarnation at noon with a pile of scholarly-looking books under his arm. She had called to him to bid him the time of day, and from that window she talked to him and smiled at him, and cast an enchantment over him and tempted him into her house.

When the winter months came to New Incarnation, and the snow ploughs trundled through the main streets of the city, Cheiron took sanctuary in the house of the woman who he had come to call his Moon Goddess. Sometimes, they left the city and took to the glistening steppes in their wintry garb, where ponies pulled their sleigh over the mantle of snow. They laughed and he kissed the frost on her bright red lips so that they brought a warmth to his own. Semele was his goddess of the moon when the sun shone over the crystalline snow or lush grass, and his harlot when the moon glided behind the clouds over New Incarnation. And he loved her.

Then, two more winters had come and gone and he was committed to the Senate House where, with luck, he was to spend all of his days seeing to the welfare of the Magnate and his Imperial problems. And with age came the end of things as he had known them, and something like a childhood dream had passed before his eyes, and Semele didn't laugh any more and, inevitably, she left him and for a long time it seemed as though the essence of his being had gone for good. A few years later, he heard that Semele was dead somewhere in the far-flung corners of the Empire in the arms of her current lover.

All those years afterwards, her death didn't hurt Cheiron Androcles as much as it should have done. Perhaps it was because he had heard about it from a business man at the Senate House, or perhaps it was that he had grown up too much since his affair. The latter was more likely since he had come to be more ruthless and temperamental in his years in the government. But now, he didn't really care about poor Semele, he had her merely to refer back to to see what unspoiled love is like. Now, he had Ylain.

The morning after their first encounter, Cheiron and Ylain wandered slowly, hand-in-hand once more, away from the village of the Cloudspeople to a hillside that he had never stood upon before during his stay. As they walked down the slope, slipping and stumbling, Ylain asked him: 'Will you be returning to your home, Cheiron?'

Cheiron shook his head. 'I doubt it. Others may come looking for me and my poor friends who died in the stratosphere, but they will not find us with their methods of watching from the sky. In a way I'm glad, now that I've found you. Perhaps more men of my kind will land here, but not for a long time because such expeditions cost a great deal of money, and the great Magnate will not finance new expeditions lightly.'

'Don't you ever wish to return home?' Ylain wanted to know, sitting down on the hillside.

Cheiron sat next to her and gazed over to Izembard, and the line of the river. 'I do miss home. I fear for my homeland because I have failed in my mission here and many people will try to take their anger out on my people, but I have a capable friend to act as guardian.'

'You were once a ruler of people? Were you like the Brotherhood in the way that you ruled them?'

Cheiron smiled at her simplicity. 'Sometimes I was forced to act as a tyrant would act. When I came to the Lands of the Aoidni, the people lived in utter degradation. Every day, hundreds died of starvation because the soil was too poor to grow crops and their animals were without sustenance. I rode into a village one day and saw a group of children scrambling for a bite of one of their own faeces. It sickened me to see a great and worthy empire so decrepit at its nerve centre. I went rebel soon afterwards and so I was forced to defy my masters to do what I believed to be the right thing. I set about expelling the Imperial authorities from the Lands of the Aoidni. We fought many battles in those days. Some were fought with different tribes of the Aoidni people in our struggle for unity. We fought on horseback with sabres of Aoidni manufacture and weapons stolen from our more advanced adversaries. It wasn't all that easy, I had to win over the confidence of the people first in various trials. I was defeated in a trial by combat for the leadership of the first tribe with whom I made contact, but their leader who had defeated me was a learned man and understood my motives. His name was Xenophon, and he is the guardian of whom I spoke.'

Ylain was silent for a long time. Then she said to him: 'I know that you will be leaving at some time or other. Gael told me about the words of Alvis, the day she interrupted you, when we were gone to the lands of the Brotherhood.'

'You are not Gael. I know that I have my quest to fulfil, but a little time spent with you cannot be harmful.' He kissed her on the cheek.

'I was so happy last night, Cheiron. I cried because I thought that I might lose you.'

'I have come to hate this burden that I have carried across the Empire, only to find that I have to bear it until I reach the place where the Lords of the Zodiac dwell, and where my questions can be answered.'

'And what will happen to me when you are fulfilling your mission?'

Cheiron answered, 'I don't know,' in a voice that she could hardly hear, and at the same time his hand rested on her bosom and his lips came down on her mouth, and he took her for his own once more.

PART THREE: BITTER SUMMER WINE

The Brotherhood

In that part of a Standard year which is governed by Lord Capricorn, Ylain gave birth to the child of Cheiron Androcles. They called her Calisto, meaning 'the fairest'. Calisto was a small baby with traces of hair the colour of her mother's and her father's eyes. Calisto's birth was regarded by the Cloudspeople as improper, being out of wedlock, but they were prepared to make allowances since Cheiron was her father and he wasn't expected to recognise all the customs of his hosts in Stoney Clouds.

Cheiron spent many happy times with Ylain and Calisto. Never once was marriage discussed, because Ylain knew that Cheiron would not commit himself to anything permanent until his quest was ended. And it was Cheiron's quest that brought about the end of these happy times. The burden still clung to Cheiron, although Ylain and her daughter were there to lighten the load. But gradually, Ylain became more and more remote, tiring of the weight of the burden which she tried to understand but could not fully share with her baby's father.

Their relationship soon came to a close. There seemed little else to say, Calisto was the last word. Ylain could fend for her baby with ease in the close community of the Cloudspeople, and so Cheiron had little to do with her upbringing. Calisto was too young to miss her father when Ylain told Cheiron that she no longer loved him, and so Cheiron did not try to argue against such a move.

Lord Aries warned Cheiron through Alvis that the time was nearing when his quest was to be resumed.

Almost as if he had expected them, Cheiron watched the thin line of riders emerge from the trees. They came down the wooded slopes and snaked out on to the flat ground between the forested rise and Stoney Clouds. Cheiron stood on Dead Man's Rock and watched the figures on their nimble mounts come towards the home of the Cloudspeople, riding two-abreast. They wore golden helmets with waving plumage and the helms shone brightly in the sunshine, casting shadows on the faces of the men. They were dressed in heavy, brown garments like coarse frocks, caught at the waist by wide leather belts suspended from which were enormous scabbards containing swords with great cruciform, elaborate hilts. The weapons were also bright and gold. Their feet were clothed in flimsy sandals and they were wrapped in heavy blue cloaks with hoods which hung at their shoulders.

Cheiron suddenly noticed that the Cloudspeople were gathering on the outcroppings which they called the Stones, and were watching the approach of the riders with excited interest, but Cheiron also noted that they seemed afraid.

Alvis walked on to Dead Man's Rock slowly and stood next to Cheiron.

'The Brotherhood?' Cheiron asked him.

Alvis nodded slowly, staring fixedly at the nearing line of blue and gold. 'I wonder what they want. It must mean serious trouble.'

The Brotherhood turned to the right and rode for a long way at the foot of Stoney Clouds before they found a steep trackway which they began to ascend. Now the jingle of the horses' trappings could be heard. The Brothers sat bolt upright and looked blankly in front of them, their red plumes swaying in the wind. Cheiron saw that on their capes were pictures of golden, winged creatures with their eyes closed and their expressions serene. They had their hands pressed together palm-to-palm and their fingertips touched. Cheiron was momentarily taken aback by the beauty of those winged creatures, but he was brought to by the chattering of the Cloudspeople as they retreated from the Stones and waited on the hilltop for the Brotherhood to arrive. The Stones were well away from the village which was concealed by hedges and bushes, and people were still coming from the direction of the settlement.

The Brotherhood lined up randomly in front of the crowd of Cloudspeople. One of them held a long, black pole on the end of which was a heavy golden cross. The man's jaw was square set and his lips tightly closed, his expression showing that he was proud to carry the emblem.

Next to the standard bearer was a man who stood out from the rest because of his manner. Whilst the others sat still and looked unblinkingly into the crowd, this man surveyed the Cloudspeople with small shifting eyes. He was tall and lean with a greying beard and a thin moustache. His eyes were surrounded by dark, lined skin which hung without life or substance from the bones of the thin face. The cracked lips beneath the beard were thin too, and pursed. Then those lips parted and the man moved his tongue around his mouth, and saliva hung thick from his small, jagged teeth.

'Vermin! *Animals!* Word has reached us that you of this wild hill have strayed wilfully from the path of righteousness by refusing to worship the true Lord God of this land. You have, instead, worshipped and believed in a false and unlawful bunch of hideous deities! This is a sin beyond forgiveness! You shall be punished, but your lives shall be spared on the condition that you give us the priest who has taught you these vile lies and blasphemies. Now! Give us your priest so that he may take his punishment!'

There was silence, but for the wind and the birds. The Cloudspeople looked at the piercing eyes with blank faces. One of the horses snorted. Cheiron glanced at Alvis.

'Very well! One by one you shall be put to death until I have your priest.' The man raised his arm and two of the Brothers rode forward from the line into the crowd, which backed away. They motioned to draw their gigantic swords from their ornate scabbards, then Alvis pushed through the crowd to the front.

'I am the Teller Alvis, and I spread the words of the great Lords of the Zodiac.'

The leader of the Brotherhood grimaced. He nudged his mount with his knees and moved slowly forwards. He drew his sword slowly and let the grim daylight reflect in the polished blade. With a sickening thud and a crack, it sank into Alvis' skull and as the blood and brains spilled from the immense gash, the old man collapsed with a groan to the grass. He looked up into the eyes of the man who had taken his life, and then sank into the pool of fresh blood.

Cheiron burst through the crowd and saw what had happened. He knelt at Alvis' side and stared at the motionless body wrapped in the robe, soaked and clinging in the blood. Cheiron touched him and then looked aghast at the dull red liquid on his fingertips. He turned his gaze to the man who had killed the old Teller, looking down with indifferent eyes, the sword still in his hand.

The man is a killer, Cheiron thought, he kills like this regularly. The Cloudspeople *expected* him to kill Alvis. Cheiron stood up slowly, the man's eyes following him with a slight glint of surprise. Suddenly, Cheiron sprang at the horse and rider and grabbed the man's forearm. He pulled, yelling, and the horse jumped as its rider toppled. Cheiron pulled the sword from the man's hand and was about to strike when he felt something hit his head, and warm blood in his hair. He tried to strike the fallen leader, but he staggered and collapsed to the ground next to him. The standard bearer raised the great golden cross on the pole to strike again, but the leader interrupted him.

'Stop! Don't kill him! Death is far to easy a way out for this one! He isn't one of these savages, otherwise he would not have dared to lay a hand on the High Father of the Brotherhood.' The man stood up, picking up his sword and wiping it on Cheiron before returning it to its scabbard. 'He will come with us. We will take also all of the children of these scoundrels, so that they may be brought up in the embrace of civilisation. As for the rest of them, they are at your mercy my brothers . . . '

Brother Kristopheros

Cheiron had vague and tormented recollections of being dragged along, stumbling, behind a horse for kilometre after kilometre up and down steep hills and along rough roads. He remembered the cries of the children as they were given the same treatment, the pain of the wound on his head and the bolt upright posture of the riders as they pulled them mercilessly along with their hands bound to long ropes.

The cries were still present, muffled and exhausted. They made patterns in the stench of the dungeon. Cheiron opened his eyes and saw firstly the stinking straw, and then he turned his head to see the darkness and the watery eyes that gleamed therein, all around. The children huddled up against the black walls and Cheiron lay sprawled in the straw in the centre of the dungeon. He remembered seeing the Great House of the Brotherhood from outside, remembered being pushed through a small door in the wall and down a narrow corridor to the dungeon. A candle flickered in one corner, its flame licking at strands of the straw, but Cheiron remembered that it was damp, and would not catch fire.

What did they do to the Cloudspeople? What have they done with the mother of my child? Cheiron raised himself to his feet and felt the tired ache in his limbs, the dampness through his clothes. He walked to where some of the children were huddled in a corner of the dank room. 'What will they do to your mother and father?' he asked one of them, a girl of about ten years.

Her face contorted with sorrow, and she forced her words through sobs. The child could only cry.

Cheiron stood and thought for a moment, feeling the ache in his skull, then he turned on his heel and surveyed the dim faces of the children. They were all looking at him, staring, wondering, some only just left babyhood. He remembered his own child.

'Calisto!' he said aloud, and looked around for his child. She was in the arms of one of the older children. The oldest of them looked about thirteen. Cheiron inspected the baby, and satisfied himself that his daughter was unharmed.

He was now at a loss for what to do. He checked the door and found that it was securely locked and was stoutly constructed of thick oak planks bound together by iron bars.

For a long time he sat crosslegged on the floor and the children gathered round him. He gave them reassurance, and when there was nothing else to say, he sat and waited for something to happen.

They came some time later, and their arrival was heralded by the harsh clanking of the ancient lock. Three burly Brothers stood one behind the other, the foremost stooping under the low arch of the doorway. They were not wearing their armour or cloaks, simply their habits. The man in the doorway carried a coiled whip, and the man at the back of the three in the corridor held a torch which cast their shadows like gargantuans into the stinking dungeon. The man looked around, moving only his large eyes, his head perched on his stooping shoulders like a solid block of stone.

After a period of nervous silence, the man in the doorway glared at Cheiron and said crisply: 'You. On your feet. Quick.' He stepped inside the doorway and indicated the corridor with the coiled whip. Cheiron got up slowly and walked into the corridor, bowing as he passed through the door. The Brother surveyed the children again and then exited the dungeon, slamming the door behind him. He locked it with a large key which he pulled from beneath the cord around his waist, and then the four of them walked down the dark, damp corridor and into the night.

The fresh evening air smelt of flowers and fruit. Cheiron felt relieved after the smell of the dungeon, but feared greatly for the children.

He was led into another door in the wall of the House and along a series of spacious, draughty corridors until they reached a long, rectangular antechamber. The floor was lined with a worn, faded carpet which had formerly been rich in its colour and texture, with golden braiding around the edges. Where there was not carpet, the flooring was of rich marble, which, Cheiron guessed, was not from this part of the world.

Through two great, brown double doors with carved handles, he was pushed into the great hall of the House. There was an overpowering, nauseous and somehow sinister smell of aged wood. It arose from the polished, cracked floorboards and the great black beams that spanned the yellow ceiling fifteen metres above their heads, and from the benches on either side of the hall that rose in steps, with long tables in front of those on the bottom-most step. Candelabras burned on the tables and illuminated the grim figures who occupied the benches with the brown hoods of their habits shadowing their bowed faces, and their hands thrust inside their sleeves.

At the far end of the hall sat the High Father of the Brotherhood. He was sitting in a large, wooden chair on a dais situated beneath the vast window with pictures in the glass. Overshadowing him was a great cross, with the gruesome effigy of a man nailed to it by his feet and wrists. Cheiron shuddered when he thought of the Cloudspeople. He controlled the shudder, and waited. The Brothers had marched him to a roughly central position in the hall, and then two of them departed leaving only the man with the whip standing at Cheiron's shoulder.

Eventually, the Father looked closely at Cheiron, then said loudly: 'Kneel, vermin!' And Cheiron felt the weight of the whip across his shoulders, and collapsed weakly to his knees. His head sagged for a moment, and then he raised it and looked into the eyes of the High Father, realising that the dampness of the dungeon had brought him out in a feverish sweat. Strands of straw clung to his filthy robes.

The Father glared down at Cheiron for a long time. His hair consisted of thin strands of oily blackness slicked across his head. His small, killer's eyes were set behind the lines of his pronounced nose. He bent forwards on the edge of his seat and looked at Cheiron who stared back, trying to look calm despite the cold sweat which he fought to control. The Father looked up at last, and snapped his fingers and pointed at the doors. Cheiron heard movement, and turned to see six of the Brothers on the row of benches to the High Father's right, near the doors, get up and leave the hall. The door closed behind them, and Cheiron turned back to the High Father.

'So,' the High Father said, splitting the silence. 'Great brave Cloudsman. Are you of the Cloudspeople? I think not, somehow. The Cloudspeople know their manners better than you. Are you a priest?'

'My name is Cheiron Androcles. I am a Senator in the Imperial government of the Second Empire of . . . '

' . . . Silence demon! I do not wish to know your status in Hell! I see your true face, O mockery of man! You are one of *their* kind! You are a follower of the false priests! You are one of their avengers. A demon from beyond the North wind! I see you, demon!'

Cheiron threw his head back and laughed, a laugh that was scornful and without amusement.

'Silence!'

The whip.

Cheiron placed his palms on the floorboards to support himself and winced at the sting of the whip.

There was clattering from the back of the hall. Cheiron peered over his shoulder and saw the six Brothers returning, carrying a massive wooden table. It was elegantly carved, but chipped and scratched and unpolished. They set it down just behind him after staggering quickly across the floorboards with the enormous weight. Four of the Brothers returned to their seats at the end of the hall, while two others walked to either side of Cheiron. They looked to the High Father, and Cheiron saw him nod, and the next moment they seized him beneath the armpits and dragged him on to the table top so that he was lying on his back on the rough surface. Metal bands were secured around his wrists and ankles and he looked up at the ceiling, the man on the cross. He couldn't see the Father, now. He heard his booming voice: 'Demon! You dared to strike me this day, soulless avenger of damned creatures! For that you must be punished. There is but one way for you to enter into humanity. You must retrieve your soul by admitting to your damned and tormented state! I know that you will not easily be able to break the spell on your wretched body so your flesh will be tortured until the Hellspirit that possesses you can no longer endure the pain and flees to let the soul of the Lord enter into you, so that you are cleansed . . . '

There was a pause, and Cheiron saw the face of the man with the whip above him. Those eyes sparkled with cruelty, and the sides of his mouth twitched.

The High Father stood up, clasping a wooden cross in his hands. Two of the Brothers went to him and draped golden lengths of material, richly embroidered with various patterns, around his neck. They retreated and Cheiron watched the High Father raise the cross to his lips and gently kiss it. He looked to the ceiling and whispered something, and then his voice boomed sanctimoniously: 'Pray you, my brothers, that the Lord in his wisdom shall grant this pitiful creature a soul. Do you renounce your present state of being, demon? Do you crave for the spirit of the Lord to enter your unworthy body?'

'The Zodiac curse you!'

There was a clank, and Cheiron turned his head to his right and saw three of the Brothers positioning a glowing brazier near to the table under the directions of the man with the whip. The handles of numerous implements protruded from the holes in the brazier.

Instruments of torture! Animals! Great Lords, their perversions are worthy of the Peacemakers of New Earth!

'In the name of the almighty God, that your inner self may be cleansed of your evil, you are delivered into the hands of the Lord's inflictor of the agonies of the flesh . . . '

The man with the whip tore away his shirt. Cheiron saw the dirty sweat matting the black hairs of his chest.

' . . . Brother Kristopheros . . . '

The whip lashed across Cheiron's chest six times. The cuts were streaked with blood, and the salt of his sweat made them sting.

'Repent your birth, demon! Curse the witch that spawned you!'

Cheiron remembered the pendant. He scanned his heaving chest and saw that it was gone. He turned his head and saw that the chain had broken and the pendant had been torn away with his shirt. He hoped that they wouldn't notice it lying there. He focussed on the images of the Zodiac, finding comfort even in the representation of Lord Satan.

'My mother wasn't a witch. My mother was a harlot, High Father, and my father a drunken noble out for a good time. I've been cursing them since birth!'

The High Father nodded to Brother Kristopheros.

Cheiron looked at the signs of the great Lords.

For half an hour he endured various tortures, passing in and out of conciousness. The tendons of his right arm were severed, and one eye put out. Eventually, his mind blanked and fled the scene of agony. They could no longer waken him.

Brother Kristopheros turned to the High Father. 'He has not repented, High Father . . . '

The High Father dropped into his chair and stroked his coarse beard. 'Then he is sentenced to the Blasted Oak, to receive a similar punishment to that of the man who you see behind me who was also unclean in the sight of the Lord. Now, get him out of here and bring fresh flowers to clear away the stench!'

The Blasted Oak

Lying there, nailed to a horizontal branch of that writhen tree, Cheiron wished that he was dead, that he had never existed. It seemed that he could no longer think as he had done before. His personality had undergone a subtle alteration, so that the fact of his being alive felt different. The memories. Androcles, the ferocious rebel of New Earth, riding into bloody victory astride a fiery steed and alongside barbarians who defied an Empire at its heart. It was like remembering another person, and it occurred to him that the man must have been the most outstanding rebel in history. And yet that place in history he had deserted. For what? Pain, physical and mental, and the forfeiture of the right to die when he pleased. Did that mean that he no longer had the right to live?

They had taken him along that climbing, winding road. They had taken him past the junction with the road from the Dale to Stoney Village, and followed the other road that climbed steeply for about a kilometre, and then turned gently through a right angle and continued to climb. Another kilometre took them to the place where the Blasted Oak stood at the roadside, on the hilltop, reaching with spidery fingers to the dark sky that had poured out doom on to the tree in ancient times. And now, there it stood with bloodied branches, carved in places with incantations instituted by the ancient Order of the Brotherhood, and wound and intertwined with age-old lore and superstition. The damned tree of death, doomed to eternal life in its almost petrified state, symbolising the soul without a place in the blessed after-life.

The storm clouds gathered in the night sky. Cheiron wondered about the day. The day had been a silhouette superimposed upon the bright realism of the pain inflicted upon his mind by the wounds which Brother Kristopheros had made. He was now blind in his left eye, and his right arm, his proud sword-arm, was useless and would soon wither as the muscles fell into disuse. Cheiron remembered the knife, the sharp silver blade that carved around in his arm until it reached the tendon, and cut through it. His eye he recalled, too. He remembered the image of the eye in a mirror or in a stream when he stooped to drink, always it had been there to guide him, to cry when he was small and there were lots of things to cry about. He felt as though he had lost a friend.

It rained, heavily. He was clad only in his rough breeches, and he was suddenly cold with the searing agony. The water washed away the saline residue on his body, washed his matted hair and his face, and Cheiron realised that the skin of his face felt unclean and unshaven.

Time crawled to a halt. The rain did not cease. Cheiron turned his head in his half-sleep, half-death, and saw the woman coming up the road from the direction of the Dale. She held her scarf tightly around her head and walked with her face looking to the rough road beneath her feet.

When she reached the foot of the tree, she looked up at Cheiron, squinting through the darkness and the rain. She saw that he was awake, alive. 'I – I heard they were doing this to you tonight. Who are you? They say you are a demon from beyond the North wind, a creature without a soul . . . '

Cheiron found the strength to speak into the face, blurred by the rain. 'Perhaps it is true that I have my soul no longer, but I am not a demon, I am a man, or the sad remnant of one who was . . . '

'My name is Kristabel. I live in the Dale. I come here to give comfort to those on this tree. All whom I have spoken to here are dead . . . they died on the tree.'

The remark didn't register in Cheiron's mind. 'Why do you come?'

'They murdered my father on this tree. My mother brought me to the Blasted Oak when they nailed him up to die. It was a night such as this, except it was thundering and lightning too. We sneaked out of the village under the curfew and came here. My father was almost dead as I stood where I'm standing now, with my mother saying: "Oh, Kristabel, after what you have seen here tonight, you will no longer fear death. Give comfort to those who are leaving on the great journey. Never forget your father, or the way he died. One day, it may be for you to send the soul of his murderer to the after-life to meet his victim. I would like to be there on that day of reckoning . . . " So I come here. Perhaps it is not what she meant for me to do, but I still come.'

'I have no will to live, but yet I cannot die. Can you comfort a man without a soul? A man who cannot die?'

'If what you say is true, then some would envy you.'

Cheiron laughed, throwing his head back until it lolled on the wood of the tree. He looked at the carbon-black sky and said loudly: 'Great Lords, can we arrange for an exchange of souls? Ha! Hahahahaha . . . '

'You seem familiar with your gods,' Kristabel said, her body saturated and shivering.

'Oh, I've come to know their ways, or at least some of them. Will you do something for me, Kristabel?'

'What?'

'I have a daughter in the Great House of the Brotherhood. She is held captive with the children of the Cloudspeople. Could you rescue her for me?'

'What is her name?'

'Calisto. Her name is Calisto. Will you . . . ?'

'I'll see what I can do. The children will be made to work on the lands of the Brotherhood, I suppose, but the babies may be given to the people of the Dale. I think that the Dalesmen will not want the children, and the babies will be more than likely put to death.'

'Save my daughter, Kristabel.'

'I will try to save your Calisto.'

'What has happened to the older Cloudspeople?'

Kristabel sighed a dismayed breath. 'The word is that most of the men have been maimed to death, and the women so dishonoured that they also chose death.'

'Suicide?'

Kristabel nodded. 'They take their own lives. Lover dies in the arms of lover, parent in the arms of the child they have raised to come of age . . . '

My Ylain too? he wondered. But no, she was no longer mine, she left me. Even now that action seems strange and sudden . . .

'Go home Kristabel. I wish to be alone now. I will return to the Dale to see my daughter tomorrow when they come to cut me down, expecting to find me dead. I will live on. Where do you live?'

'At the horse farm. The farm is called Ferntree.'

'Thank you. Goodbye.'

'Goodbye, man. I hope that you find your soul one day.' And with that she walked away, down the road in the direction she had come.

Cheiron watched her go until she was obscured by the night. Will my soul and with it my right to life and death ever return to me? When the quest is fulfilled? Oh, Lords, give me your help . . .

Kristabel

In the morning, they came and pulled out the nails, and Cheiron was allowed to fall to the ground at the roadside. They were surprised that he was still alive, but they didn't wait long and they went away on their horses, back towards the village, expecting him to die soon.

For a long time, Cheiron lay motionless at the roadside. After the milky sun had washed the sky and rose to noonday, Cheiron heaved his body up with great difficulty. They had taken his footwear. The wounds in his feet and hands bled. Slowly, painfully he began the long walk back to the Dale.

It took him several hours to reach the Dale, resting occasionally. He followed the road until he came to the junction of the crooked road near the Great House of the Brotherhood. The Great House towered over the little cottages and farmhouses which lined the street.

Ferntree farm was a modest little farm. The farmhouse was really a small cottage, huddled in between two rather grander farm buildings. Cheiron remembered mistily that Kristabel had said that the farm dealt in horses. He went through the open gateway and into the farmyard. The farmyard was enclosed by stables and there was an overwhelming smell of horse manure.

Cheiron looked around. There seemed to be no one there. Cheiron turned on his heel and then walked to a nearby stable door and looked in. There was a man asleep on the hay. He was a tall, thin-looking character with long brown hair. He wore a wide-brimmed hat that shaded his eyes. His clothes were practical and not inexpensive, but untidy.

Cheiron felt suddenly sick. Pain flooded through his arm

and burned in his ruined eye. He turned from the stable door and threw up a pool of vomit. The noise of Cheiron's agonised sickness awoke the man sleeping in the stable, who came to the door. Cheiron fell to his knees as the attack of pain in his arm and eye grew worse. The man came quickly out of the stable and bent down to Cheiron.

'Who are you?' the man enquired. He looked at Cheiron's feet and hands. 'The Blasted Oak,' he murmured. 'You'd better come along into the house.'

The man helped Cheiron slowly around to the back door of the cottage and entered the building. The hall was richly panelled with wood, and shiny metal ornaments were hanging from the walls alongside abstract pictures in dazzling colours.

They went into the living room of the house, with a small dining table in its centre. They had to lower their heads to enter through the door into the living room, the ceiling of which wasn't a great deal higher.

Cheiron was laid down on a long, aged sofa. After putting Cheiron there, the man hurried out of the room and into another. Soon afterwards, Kristabel came into the living room followed by the man who had brought Cheiron in. She walked over to him slowly and looked down at him. Through the agony that shrouded his sight, Cheiron saw her dark eyes and pale, smooth face with its small, delicate nose and lips. Her hair was dark and brushed around her oval face like a shadow caressing a fine portrait. Kristabel smiled, a delicate smile. 'You were right, then,' she said in a low voice.

Cheiron attempted to return the smile, but the pain once more swamped his body and his face betrayed his torment.

Kristabel turned to the man, who clutched his hat in his hands and looked down at Cheiron with dark blue eyes set into deep sockets above protruding cheekbones over which ruddy, rough skin was pulled tightly, stretching down to thin, cracked lips. 'Fetch me some hot water, bandages and the medicine chest from the kitchen, please, Cailean.'

Cailean scurried away into the kitchen and returned after a few moments with the things that Kristabel had requested. Kristabel then washed the wounds and treated them with medicine from her store. After treating the wounds, she bandaged them and then dressed Cheiron in some clean wrappings which smelt of freshness and cleanliness.

Cheiron lapsed into unconsciousness as Kristabel was applying the medicine, and he stayed in that state for three days.

Sometimes he would awaken for short periods and have liquid poured down his throat. He tried on two occasions to enquire after his daughter, but each time he spewed up his liquid meal.

Cheiron felt himself returning to the land of the living in the middle of the night on the third day. Consciousness came to him like a breeze on its travels. There were excited dreams, and the sound of his own heartbeat was loud in his ears. There was a breath of springtime on New Earth, a taste of the autumn leaves and a chill of winter and then the blessed awakening. The darkness of the room. I only have one eye . . . one eye . . . Cheiron opened his mouth. It was dry and tasted stale and unhealthy. He relaxed his tense breathing and moved his head around, looking into the darkness of the room. Slowly, vaguely, he began to recall the trek from the Blasted Oak to Ferntree farm. He remembered the stables and the man Cailean. He remembered Kristabel, and then Calisto.

For the rest of the night, Cheiron slept a natural sleep, and when Kristabel came to him the next morning to see how he was, he lay awake with his good eye wide open and staring up at the low, beamed roof. 'I'm glad to see that you are recovering,' she said.

'You need not have worried, I am not yet ready to die. Did you find my daughter, Kristabel?'

'Yes, yes. Calisto is in my room. The other children are being made to work on the lands of the Brotherhood. The smallest ones are being cared for by the children themselves. They will probably die without their mothers, though.'

'There has been so much death of late. There is too much talk of death and the dead. Too much torment.'

'I am used to death. I used to fear death before my father was murdered on the Blasted Oak. Now, death doesn't bother me much at all.'

Cheiron sighed heavily and turned his head to look out of the little window above the sofa. From his position he could only see the sky. The day looked warm, but fresh with towering white clouds in the sky. 'The perpetual summer of Acima,' Cheiron murmured.

'Pardon?'

'Oh, it's nothing. It's just that where I come from the seasons are very short and in his lifetime a man may see many summers, winters, springtimes and falls.'

'What is the winter like?'

'It depends whereabouts in the world you are. In my homelands the winters are not too severe as far as the temperature goes, but we do get extremes of weather. In the far north of the planet New Earth, around the great city of New Incarnation, there is snow and ice in the wilderness and on the streets of the city. The snow is white and very cold and it hangs from the roofs of houses. In the autumn, just before the winter, the leaves turn golden brown and fall from the trees with each gust of wind, and the trees are bare and black when the snows come.'

'What happens in the springtime?'

'In the springtime, the leaves grow again, and the flowers from beneath the ground, and the snow melts to feed the fast mountain streams so that they swell and rush in great torrents through the rocks and soil.'

'And then summer comes again.'

Cheiron nodded.

'It must be marvellous to see the seasons pass you by that way. I would like to visit your home world some time, but I don't think it is possible.'

Cheiron smiled. 'My home world is a long, long way from here, way up beyond the clouds, beyond your stormy sky.'

They were silent for a long time, then Kristabel said: 'Would you like to see your daughter, Cheiron?'

'Yes, yes I would like that. Is she well?'

'She is unharmed. She is very quiet, almost thoughtful. She is a wonderful child, Cheiron.'

Cheiron smiled, almost with pride. 'It gladdens me to know that you like Calisto. But I do not wish to impose upon you.'

'Helping one who has been dealt with by the Brotherhood is no imposition, Cheiron.'

'Is Cailean your husband, Kristabel?'

Kristabel pulled off the sheets and helped Cheiron unsteadily to his bandaged feet. 'No, Cailean is not my husband. Cailean helps me run the farm and looks after the welfare of the stable-hands. Cailean is efficient, and, I feel, considers himself to be my man. I suppose he is in a way. He is the only man I have been able to trust of late. These are not easy times.'

Kristabel helped Cheiron out of the living room of the cottage and up the carved wooden stairs. They went into her pleasant bedroom and walked across a soft carpet to a small cot in which Calisto lay asleep. Cheiron bent down and kissed the child on the forehead, and after staring at her in thoughtful silence for a few moments, turned his attention to the room.

On the walls were pictures in bright colours. There was a rabbit, dressed in human clothes and holding a timepiece. There was a little blonde girl in a red dress with bright blue eyes, and there was a cat without a body. The cat was grinning. On one wall marched a regal procession headed by a grand queen who looked with distaste at two fellows who seemed to be painting some flowers.

'What strange pictures you have,' Cheiron remarked.

Kristabel stood at his elbow, giving him support. 'They are from very old stories. I am told that the stories date back before the Holocaust. The stories were called "Alice in Wonderland". The pictures have been handed down through generations of our family, like this house and the farm itself.'

Cheiron looked into the scenes depicted on the walls of the bedroom, the grinning cat that reminded him of the way things seemed the night that he had 'proposed' to Gael. He turned his attentions back to the cot. 'Did you have any trouble in getting her out of the Great House?'

'I gave them my best horse in exchange for the child.'

'Oh, I'm sorry. I'll – er – work to repay the debt.'

'A horse is a small price to pay for a human life, Cheiron.'

Cheiron smiled into her eyes. 'It's just that in my homelands we hold our mounts in a somewhat higher esteem.'

'We too value our horses. The farm is my living. I provide the mounts for the Brotherhood. Now and then I purchase breeding stock from the Cloudspeople. A lot of the farmers around here get their workhorses from Stoney Clouds.'

Cheiron suddenly thought of Ylain and Alvis and the people he had known on Stoney Clouds. What is it like up there now? Are they all dead? Ylain is my child's mother. It should mean more to me, and yet perhaps I have been through too much physical pain of late to be able to feel any emotion. I was warned by the Lords . . . By the Zodiac, she's the child's mother. I owe her something. Love – respect. It was she who ended our relationship, but still I cannot shun my responsibility, lest I become less than a man.

'Cheiron . . . ?' Kristabel interrupted his thoughts gently.

'I was thinking about her mother . . .'

'You loved her?'

'I think perhaps I did. I no longer shared her life for a long time before the Brotherhood came to Stoney Clouds but there is an obligation. Do you think I might be able to borrow a horse one day and visit Stoney Clouds?'

'I suppose so. I'll come with you, but we won't be going until you're well enough.'

His eye was not as bad as he thought it would be. It was swollen and scorched and the eyeball was completely ruined. He touched the branded cross on his cheek gingerly. With his good eye, Cheiron inspected the face in a mirror. He sighed, but saw that, apart from his left eye, he hadn't changed a great deal. His hair was longer, his teeth yellowed, but his face was about the same. He glanced down at his right arm, hanging limp and useless at his side. He wondered what the Brotherhood would do if they knew that he was alive and living beneath their noses in the Dale. The Brotherhood! I owe the Brotherhood something. I forget that I promised them their destruction, but now I remember I shall have my revenge.

Cheiron replaced the bandage on his eye and went out of the kitchen and into the living room where Kristabel sat in one of the old chairs brushing her hair. He had been with her and Cailean for that part of the Standard Year governed by Taurus, the Bull Lord. Kristabel looked up and saw him standing in the doorway. 'Hello. How do you feel this morning?'

'Thank you, the pain is nearly gone. Do you think these coverings can be removed today?'

'I should think so.' She put the brush down on the arm of her chair and came to him and began to untie the knots on the bandage around his eye. 'It looks better,' she reported. 'Of course, you'll never see out of it again.'

Cheiron nodded. 'Will the tendons of my arm and hand ever mend?'

'I doubt it. The Brotherhood's methods are thorough and time-tested. The tendons are probably severed right the way through. One or two of them might knit back together.'

'You seem to know much about healing, Kristabel.'

'My mother taught me what I know,' Kristabel answered, undoing the bandages on his arm gingerly.

The smell of the ointments touched Cheiron's nostrils. 'Was your mother a doctor?'

'A what?'

'Did she heal many people in return for money or gifts?'

'Oh, no. If there was sickness in the village, they would come to her, but she asked for no payment. She learned medicine through experience. When my mother was young, there were frequent raids from Izembard and the Brotherhood had many casualties.'

Cheiron moved to a chair when Kristabel had removed the bandage and sat down. She followed him and sat on the arm of the chair inspecting the wounded limb. 'What sort of weapons did the raiders use, do you know?'

'They use rods with weird attachments that spit rays of heat and burn people to death. They say that the raiders have harnessed the sun in their fire rods, because the rays look like narrow sunbeams but they are much, much hotter.'

'We have similar weapons on New Earth and throughout the Empire. But how do the Brotherhood combat these raiders with only swords?'

Kristabel began to remove the bandage on Cheiron's right hand. 'The fire rods can only shoot their rays once, then the raiders are like the bees, they sting once and then die . . . by the swords of the Brotherhood unless they escape.'

'Is it true that they only steal virgins?'

'Yes, why?'

'How can they tell so quickly which maidens are virgins?'

'There is a voice in the mist when it comes, the voice of the evil Countess of Izembard. It's a strange voice and it is such that those who are pure cannot flee, though they want to, and a red blotch appears on their forehead.'

'Have many been stolen?'

'Very many. We don't know what they do with them in Izembard, though. They only take those beyond puberty, so they might use them as we use breeding horses here. It's a hideous thought, but that's the best theory I've heard. We haven't had a raid for a long time. People are saying that they're all dead in Izembard or else they are too fearful of the Brotherhood to come to the district.'

Cheiron looked at his white hand resting in Kristabel's. 'Which part of the Dale do they usually visit?'

'They've never been known to attack us here because of the Great House. Stoney Village is very vulnerable to their attacks, and likewise Stoney Clouds. There are one or two minor settlements which have been devastated once or twice during raids.'

Cheiron was quiet for a long time whilst Kristabel removed the bandages around his other hand and feet, then he said: 'I must enter Izembard some day soon.'

'Why, Cheiron?' She stopped looking at the wounds and looked up at Cheiron instead.

'To pursue my quest. I have told you of it often enough.'

'And your daughter? What about Calisto?'

'May I leave her with you?'

Kristabel stood up, holding the bandages. 'Yes, I will care for her.'

'Can we visit Stoney Clouds today?'

'Tomorrow. You must get used to your disabilities. We will go tomorrow morning.'

'I will prepare for that time, exercise my stiff muscles.'

Cheiron wondered, as Kristabel left the room, what he would do if he found Ylain was dead.

Ylain Revisited

They led the horses out of the farm gate early in the morning when darkness still persisted and the air stung cold and moist. Cheiron wore a long, heavy green cloak fastened with a brooch at the shoulder, and over his useless right arm a black leather gauntlet which reached above the elbow. His left eyc was covered by a patch secured about his head with a leather thong to hide the distorted flesh. Beneath the cloak he wore a rough brown jerkin over a richly embroidered shirt which matched the breeches, tucked into the large, soft leather boots with generous turnovers.

Kristabel led the way along a dark and crooked street, blending into the darkness with her long black cape and hood. Her polished riding boots reached above her knees and disappeared beneath a heavy smock of purple material. Cheiron followed her out of the Dale.

After a long walk, they were out of earshot of the Great House and took to horseback, riding steadily towards Stoney Clouds.

They took the long tortuous route to Stoney Clouds, to avoid passing through Stoney Village itself. It was important for Cheiron's stay in the Dale to remain secret lest the Brotherhood should hear of it.

It was a long road, and by the time they reached the approach to the hill, the line of broken black clouds was visible on the bright and hazy horizon. They rode steadily up the steep track which entered some trees, between sandstone walls, until they reached the top, where it levelled out and went winding towards a cluster of bushes and a rickety gateway which gave access to Stoney Clouds proper. This they cantered through and entered the large, sloping rectangular field in which the horses of the Cloudspeople grazed. They followed the muddy track along the bottom of the field and passed through a gap in a thicket to enter the field in which was situated the village of the Cloudspeople.

The very atmosphere of the place in the watery light of the morning was oppressive. Most of the huts were gone, leaving only burnt grass and scorched earth where they had stood. Cheiron and Kristabel halted at the end of the field and looked at the scene. The Cloudspeople looked collectively like a single body still suffering from the shock of a disaster. There were few of them, and they slept outside in the rain or limped around on the wet grass dressed in filthy rags. There was no laughter, no tears.

The two riders urged their mounts forwards and stopped at the perimeter of the cluster of huts. The Cloudspeople halted and looked at them. Their eyes contained no greeting, no feeling; their gaze was not even enquiring. They just looked. With his single good eye, Cheiron scanned the faces, looked beyond them and saw a woman bent over a tub of water in which she was scrubbing some clothes. Her hair was the colour of the harvest. The long, brown animal skin dress did not conceal the curve of her hips, nor the shapeliness of her thighs. Cheiron dismounted and handed the reins to Kristabel. His horse began to munch at the grass underfoot.

Cheiron walked through the gathering of Cloudspeople, past friends who were now strangers. They stank. Many were mutilated and crippled. He stopped a couple of metres behind Ylain. He knew she could sense his presence. She stopped her scrubbing and seemed to bow her head to cry into the tub of water. Cheiron came close up to her and touched her on her shoulder. She did not respond, so he turned her around to face him, and a wave of horror swept through his body. Her small eyes were almost completely closed. They were swollen and battered, and Cheiron could see beneath the right eyelid a scratched and bleeding eyeball. Her nose was broken, and covered with ugly scabs at the end, damaged so that mucus flowed freely on to her smashed and battered upper lip. There was no lower lip, and her teeth were broken, blackened and already diseased. Her soft skin was scarred and bruised. One of her ears had been torn.

Cheiron's jaw hung low with horror. 'What . . . have they . . . ' He clasped hold of her, pulling her against him, holding her tight, not wanting ever to release her from his warming hold. He sobbed profusely on her shoulder. Then she pushed him away.

'Go,' she uttered in an unrecognisable voice.

'Ylain, I – I – I'm sorry. Sorry.' He didn't know what he was sorry for.

'Go.'

'Calisto is well. She is . . . well. Great Lords! Why have they done this to you?'

'You must . . . go . . . '

Cheiron felt someone touch his shoulder. He turned and saw Kristabel.

'You can do no good here, Cheiron. Ylain knows that. Do as she says, let's return to the Dale.'

Cheiron stood perfectly still for a long time. Ylain turned away from him and began to scrub the clothes again. She heard him turn and walk away. For a moment she stopped what she was doing and then went at her work more furiously than before.

They rode back down the hill towards the Dale when it was almost noon. They rode in silence, as Cheiron found himself unable to respond to Kristabel's reassurances. They turned a bend slowly and the lands of the Brotherhood, the Great House and its surrounding villages were visible in the distance. But they saw only the four men who stood in the middle of the road at the bottom of the hill holding their horses by the reins. As Cheiron and Kristabel drew closer, the four members of the Brotherhood drew their swords and waited. Cheiron recognised the High Father amongst them. Cheiron and Kristabel slowed and stopped before they reached them. The High Father stepped forwards.

'So, demon, you have more than one life! You return to cast your enchantments upon an innocent woman of the Dale. This time I am going to make sure that you shall cast no more enchantments, demon! The woman shall spend a few days on our lands to cleanse her soul, but you shall not be cleansed of your evil for it has so stained your mind that it cannot be removed. You will die here and now.'

The Hermits

The Brothers, swords naked, left their horses and surrounded the two riders. The Father stepped closer and placed his sword against Cheiron's belly. 'Dismount,' he ordered.

Cheiron hesitated for a moment, then moved to dismount. A split second later, he tugged hard on the reins of his horse, making him rear up, hoofs flailing. The High Father was sent sprawling to the ground. The other Brothers moved in, but Cheiron brought his mount down on top of them. He then wheeled the horse round, across to the other side of the road, charging full tilt at the boundary fence separating the road from the lands of the Brotherhood. Kristabel followed suit and they were over in a flurry of leaves and twigs and heading over the steeply inclined field.

The Brothers were not slow to follow, and pursued the two fugitives on to the track at the foot of the Hermit's wood. One of the Brothers broke off and sped towards the Great House in the middle distance to fetch assistance.

They pounded along the track, the mud spattering up from the horses' hooves and their capes flapping in the wake of their flight. Strange noises began to issue from the trees as they rode along the track, and then quite suddenly there were several white streaks which slashed down from the trees and plucked the riders from their mounts, but for Kristabel whose horse stumbled and slipped on the mud and staggered downhill to recover itself.

Cheiron felt a whiplash drag him through the air like a lasso and then he was flung down into the bracken at the foot of a tall tree. He rolled on to his back and saw that three Brothers had also been flicked into the trees and were surrounded by a group of small men dressed in rough brown clothes and holding bows and arrows and swords. He heard footsteps, and he turned his head dizzily to see an arrow pointing down into his face. The man holding the weapon gestured, and Cheiron obeyed by getting to his feet. He looked out into the field and saw a group of about twenty Brothers come charging up the hill towards the wood. Kristabel's mount was out of control despite her expert tugging at the reins and she careered into the Brotherhood. They took charge of her, and then continued their assault on the trees. A hail of arrows drove them back like lightning bolts, and after three successive attempts to get near the wood they gave up and galloped back towards the Great House.

Cheiron feared that Kristabel might have been struck by one of the arrows, but he caught a glimpse of her as she sped towards the Great House, pulled along by the Brotherhood. Cheiron turned to the man with the bow and arrow. 'You are the outlaws of Hermit's Wood?'

'Come with me.'

The man led Cheiron into the depths of the wood. From all around, men came down from the trees and forced the three members of the Brotherhood to their feet and then up the steep hill to a destination somewhere deep in the trees.

Slowly they clambered a steep hill still heavily wooded, often crawling on hands and knees, until they reached a track which led along the top of the hill. They walked along this until they stood over what looked to be a sheer sandstone face which dropped about half the height of the hill. Around this they were led, and then down so that they emerged at last at the encampment of the outlaws which consisted of three large caves cut into the rockface. Outside the caves was a shelf of muddy ground, perched on the edge of a steep hill of slimy mud which looked almost impossible to scale.

The people of the encampment were gathered around a cooking fire outside the caves, watching several fowls being turned on a spit. One of the men who had brought the prisoners stepped forward and spoke to the large, shaggy-haired individual who sat closest to the fire. 'Look what we've brought you, Michael. Three nice fat Brethren and another of the Dalesmen. I think the good Brothers were pursuing our other visitor.'

The man addressed as 'Michael' stood up and walked over to where Cheiron stood, wrapped in his cloak, muddied and wet.

'You have some quarrel with the Brotherhood, man?' he asked gruffly.

Cheiron looked around and then nodded slowly.

'He is a demon!' the Father suddenly burst out. He broke free from the outlaws who restrained him and looked into the faces of the men who sat around the fire. 'Hear me? He is a demon! He will take your souls and fry them to a crisp and then eat of them! Kill him! Kill him and there may then be hope for you in our society! Hear me? Kill – ' The High Father was suddenly rolling in the mud. Michael stood over him.

'We want no part in your "society" or your killing,' Michael said. He turned back to Cheiron. 'What is your quarrel with the Brotherhood?'

Cheiron touched the patch on his eye, the brand on his cheek. 'This,' he said, and then held up and dropped and let swing his useless arm. 'And this. And more; they mutilated my child's mother on Stoney Clouds. That man grovelling in the mud before you is the High Father of the Brotherhood. He is the only demon around these parts.'

There was a gasp of surprise from the outlaws. 'A lucky catch,' Michael said. He looked again at Cheiron. 'By your clothes, you are a Dalesman, not a Cloudsman.'

'I am neither. My name is Cheiron Androcles, and I am from a far-off land.'

'Space traveller?'

Cheiron was taken aback by the knowledge implied by the question. 'Yes, that is correct. I am, or was, Senator of the government of the Second Empire of New Earth. But, how . . . '

'You can ask questions later. You are safe, but what am I to do with these wretches? Have you any ideas, Senator Androcles?'

Cheiron swallowed, looked at the men and looked around at the faces of the outlaws. The face of Ylain was burned on to his memory as clearly as the brand on his left cheek, but still hot and stinging with a greater agony. 'Kill them,' he said.

The outlaws were silent. Cheiron turned his head to look into the eyes of the three members of the Brotherhood. There was no fear in their eyes. Cheiron had expected fear, particularly from the younger of the trio, but there was none.

Michael took a sword from one of the men and pressed it into Cheiron's left hand. He gestured for the cluster of outlaws to widen into a semi-circle, leaving Cheiron and the Brothers standing in the space. 'Are you man enough to take their lives yourself, Cheiron Androcles? Ponder your hate, Senator. Can you kill these men in hatred?'

Cheiron moved to the High Father and placed the tip of the blade on his breast, positioning it to push the metal through the man's heart. 'I think not of hate,' he said, seeing all the time Ylain's face, 'but of love.' He drew back the blade to strike.

'– Then kill the young one first,' Michael broke in.

They think that I would not, but I have not forgotten Ylain, he thought.

'You make a game of death, of execution . . .'

Michael did not move, nor change his expression, nor speak.

Cheiron's cape swirled, his body turned, his muscles obeyed the signal to reflex. The long blade plummeted into the young man's breast, penetrating the heart cleanly with the force of an expert thrust. The man yelled in pain, and collapsed into the mud where he curled and was still, the breeze fluttering the plume of his helmet. As he fell, the blade slid out of the wound and blood glistened in the daylight which entered through the canopy of leaves far above.

Cheiron looked at Michael. The High Father got to his knees and uttered a prayer for his Brother, and then looked accusingly at Cheiron. 'You killed this youth in cold blood, demon.'

'Think about those words, High Father,' Cheiron said. 'Think on them carefully. Remember the day you came to Stoney Clouds and put a sword through the old Teller's head. I do believe that you take pleasure in your killing. Think about the innocent women that your brave Brothers raped and butchered in the name of your god. Think about it. As far as I'm concerned, you may keep your miserable life. You and your friend may return to the Great House, if that is what Michael wishes. But always remember this day, High Father.'

Michael stepped forward. 'I will send them back if you so wish, Cheiron Androcles. I have never seen a man kill as you did in cold blood just then. Does it take much courage?'

'Not courage, sir, just sufficient reason. They are destroyers. It is a great failing of humanity that in the end we must always answer destruction with destruction. I have said before, I take no glory in death.'

Michael clapped Cheiron on the shoulder and took the sword from his hand. 'You are a wise man, my friend. My men will see to these. You will eat with us.'

Cheiron bent down and took the dead man's sword. 'I would

like to keep this,' he said, examining the massive blade and golden hilt.

'Keep it by all means, Senator. Now, come and feast with us.'

Cheiron followed Michael and sat down near the fire, and watched the outlaws usher the two Brothers out, while two others carried the body away. When they had vanished into the trees, Cheiron turned his attention to Michael. He was a large, thick-set man with thick wild hair and glassy but penetrating grey eyes. His features were broad and rough.

'So, Senator, how do you come to be in the Dale?' Michael asked of Cheiron.

'It is a long story. In parts I am hardly sure myself. I came here on a mission for a high-ranking official of the Imperium, but my main preoccupation is the pursuit of a quest laid out by the Lords of the Zodiac. I know that it sounds fantastic, but that's how it is. There were four of us who came, but my friends died in an accident. They were not directly involved in my quest.'

'And you spoke of "the mother of your daughter" . . . ?'

'A woman of Stoney Clouds called Ylain. She was mutilated almost beyond recognition by the Brotherhood . . . I only saw her today, saw what they'd done.'

'You spent some time with the Cloudspeople?' A woman handed Michael a hunk of meat which he tore in half and gave half to Cheiron.

Cheiron chewed the fowl, then replied: 'Yes, quite a long time as a matter of fact. I never married Ylain, though.'

'We have had many Tellers here,' Michael said, the grease of the meat running down his bristly chin. 'They taught me much about the omniverse and the empires and confederacies and so on. I think they were surprised to find one to interested to learn such things. It is the custom of my ancestors to accept new ideas, though. You may have heard of Michael the Hermit before. He is a member of the Brotherhood who – '

'I know the story, Michael.'

'Then you know that they think that the old man is still alive. That is partially true, because he is alive in me and my men to a certain extent.'

Cheiron fondled the hilt of the sword that he had taken from the man he had just killed. He chewed on the meat thoughtfully.

'Are you familiar with the legends of the Dale?' Michael asked.

'I know a little. I know the legends about the great birds and their eggs, the rise of the Brotherhood, the "Holocaust".'

'I find our legends fascinating,' Michael said. 'They can be interpreted easily if you think about it. A spaceship was sent from your world and it came to Acima, where it landed two or three landing craft. The spaceship later came to be remembered as a bird, and the landing vehicles as eggs. The people came out of the landing craft and set about cultivating the Dale and making it habitable. Some commercially minded people set about building Izembard, an industrial complex to produce some unknown commodity. The people who came here worshipped their god, the god of the Brotherhood. But as time went on, things began slowly to be forgotten or immersed in legend, and the Great House, built to be a temple of worship for the god of these people, became a place of tyranny and cruelty as the holy order misinterpreted the teachings of the book of their Lord.'

Cheiron had not been paying very much attention. Kristabel was in his thoughts. 'You have learned much from the Tellers, Michael.'

'I am quite a quick learner. There is more to come. You say you know of the Holocaust, Cheiron? . . . Cheiron?' Michael broke into his thoughts.

'What? Oh, yes. Yes, I know of it.'

'Well, there is an explanation for that. By this time, Izembard had been so polluted by the commercialists, that the people therein were horrible to behold. But Izembard had little to do with the Holocaust. It is most likely that the Holocaust was a war which began on your homeworld between two nations, and spread to the colonies of your people throughout the galaxy. On New Earth, the war is called the Apocalypse, here it is called the Holocaust. So you see? It all fits nicely into place. You agree? Senator, are you listening?'

'A thousand apologies. I have things on my mind.'

'I'm sorry if I bore you, my friend Cheiron. I get so few people to talk to when there are no Tellers.'

'I am greatly interested in your legends too, but at the moment I have my troubles to contemplate.'

Michael threw away the bone from which he had chewed the meat of the fowl. 'Something bothers you?'

'Yes. The Brotherhood captured the woman I was with. I sit here eating and talking whilst she has been taken to the Great House.'

'Did they say what they were going to do with her?'

'Yes, they said that they were going to make her work on their lands. They said that I'd enchanted her and blackened her soul . . . '

'She was a Daleswoman?'

'Yes.'

'Then it is very unlikely that they will harm her. The Brotherhood are respected by the Dalesfolk. The power of the Brotherhood is, to a large extent, based upon the respect of the upper class of the land, they being the Dalesmen. They will simply make her work to "cleanse her soul".'

Cheiron threw away the bone of his meat. 'Thank you, Michael. May I find a place in the trees to watch the lands with? I'd like to be sure that she is well.'

'Of course, my friend. There are many good trees for watch-posts. We observed your being chased from high in our natural roof. You may join one of my men on watch duty. Tonight we will have a feast. There is a minstrel in the Dale, and the word is that he will be coming to sing for us tonight if he can get away unseen. He is from the High Table of Bards and Tellers.'

'I shall return for your feast.'

Michael ordered one of his men to take Cheiron to where a lonely watcher sat astride a thick branch with his bow slung over his shoulder and a quiver of arrows at his side.

As Cheiron sat and looked out across the Dale, half listening to the conversation of the watchman, he wondered who could have let the Brotherhood know of his journey to Stoney Clouds with Kristabel. The thought was soon swept aside by relief when he saw Kristabel on the land, helping to plant seed. He watched her for a long time, until she left the land and returned to the Great House. Cheiron returned to the encampment at nightfall in an angry mood, angry because of what they had done to Ylain, what they were making Kristabel do, angry because he didn't know who told the Brotherhood of their journey, and angry most of all because he could think of nothing to do about it.

The Love Warrior

'Behold the Love Warrior,
Mighty in the heart,
But weakened in the soul.
Behold the blade,
The blade that thirsts
For a bleeding heart,
To repay the loss of the slayer . . . '

When the minstrel had finished, Cheiron looked into his grey-blue eyes. 'A bard of the High Table has a song for every occasion,' he remarked.

The young, blonde minstrel smiled at Cheiron. 'A song for joy, a song for grief, a song for mourning, a tale of vengeance . . . '

Cheiron grinned, slightly drunk.

'Sing for us more!' one of the outlaws cried.

The minstrel touched the strings of his instrument, let his thumb roll over them, sending the notes reverberating through the corridors of the minds of those who listened. He sang the song loudly and expertly, so that the sound of his voice echoed out across the Dale in contrast with the chants of the Brotherhood in their Great House.

The drink put the Hermits to sleep in the early hours of the morning. Stephanos, the minstrel, went into one of the caves and laid out his fur rugs and set his instrument down at his side. He settled down to sleep and closed his eyes, relaxing his mind. Not long afterwards, he was awakened by the sound of footsteps rustling in the fallen leaves scattered about the floor of the cave. Stephanos opened his eyes and saw the large figure of Cheiron Androcles stagger in through the doorway. Cheiron looked around, then turned and put his head out of the door and was violently sick. He came back into the cave, wiping his mouth. He walked unsteadily closer, but his voice was firm when he spoke, unaffected by the liquor.

'How did you arrive here?' he asked.

'You are drunk, my friend. Go to sleep and we will talk in the morning.'

'You must answer me. How did you get here?'

'I sky-dived from a spacecraft. Go to sleep.'

'I don't want to sleep,' Cheiron answered angrily. 'Tell me, when are you leaving and how?'

'I leave when the High Table sends another ship, and that won't be for another four or five Standard years. Now, for goodness' sake go to sleep or at least let me sleep.'

Cheiron walked to the corner of the cave which had been allotted to him previously, and sat down and toyed with the sword he had taken from the dead man. Suddenly he cried, cried like a child for no reason he could think of but he was still so weak from the terrible things that had happened to him. Hot tears streamed down his cheeks and made his shirt damp. He crawled over to where the minstrel lay, still holding the sword absent-mindedly. He gave the minstrel a shake. 'Someone betrayed me, someone informed the Brotherhood of my journey to Stoney Clouds.'

'Yes, yes. I've heard how you came to be here. Look, everything'll be fine if you just try to sleep.'

'Liar!' Cheiron burst out, making the others in the cave stir in their sleep. 'You are a liar,' he said more quietly. To him, in his disturbed state, no one was to be trusted. Least of all this stranger, this Teller. 'It will not be all right.'

'You blind and drunken fool! It was the woman's man who told them! The one called Cailean. You should have known better than to have tried to steal Kristabel away from him! What are you, Senator Androcles? You typify the corrupt hierarchy of New Earth. You don't own these people's lives, Senator. Why did you come to Acima? You make love to half the female population of the Dale, and do not shoulder your responsibilities. Why?'

'How dare you accuse me of such things!' Cheiron stood up, his honour stained, and raised the sword to strike at the minstrel. Stephanos sprang to his feet, deflecting the blow with his elbow and then plunged his taut fingers into Cheiron's armpit. Cheiron screamed in pain and fell to the floor, dropping the sword. He tried to clutch his heart with his right hand, but remembered that it could not respond. He tried awkwardly with his left.

Stephanos returned to his bed and tossed over and relaxed his muscles. Cheiron, sprawled on the floor, heaved himself up as well as he could and sobbed again. He looked into the sleeping, drunken face of one of the outlaws, but there was no one to hear his outpourings, the despair of a man whose every action was blighted and misunderstood on this strange planet.

Sleep descended, and his mind cleared as the dreams came to him, or, rather, drunken nightmares. Then there was something else. He dreamt that he had walked through the trees and he had come across a steaming lake of blood. He walked into the lake and began to walk in the direction of the other side. It got gradually deeper until it reached his thighs, his waist. He looked down into the lake and saw beneath the blood faces. He saw Ylain lying there, and as he walked past her she shrivelled suddenly with age and turned to dust. He walked further, and looked around him and saw the Brotherhood standing on the banks of the lake, reaching out with their hands to help him out, but he turned his face and walked on until the blood came to his chest. Then he saw Kristabel in the lake, and he heard her voice crying out for help. He sank below the surface and felt himself being pulled down, until the scarlet blood turned darker as the light penetrated the depths less and less. He felt his lungs bursting, and he thrashed around in the blood, but he only exhausted himself, and he was squirming to free himself when the blood filled his lungs, and he awoke.

He was covered in a cold sweat. He was cold all over, with no rugs wrapped around his body to give him warmth. Grey-blue daylight entered through the entrance of the cave. His head throbbed. His mouth was dry, and his breath foul. He lifted himself and crawled to his corner, where he wrapped himself in his furs and sat and waited for someone else to stir. He looked across to where the minstrel had slept, and saw that he had gone. He heard faint voices and footsteps outside in the early morning air, and shortly afterwards the smell of cooking.

The Lake of Blood

When he had eaten, Stephanos the minstrel came into the cave and collected his furs into a bundle which he secured with cord. He slung the bundle over his shoulder with the cord and over the other shoulder he put his musical instrument. Cheiron watched him thoughtfully, still sitting in the corner of the cave. The minstrel was about to exit the cave when Cheiron called him back.

'What is it?' Stephanos asked.

'About last night . . . '

'Yes?'

'You said it was Cailean who told the Brotherhood about Kristabel and me going to Stoney Clouds.'

'Yes, he did. Look, I'm sorry if I was a bit sharp with you last night, but you were drunk and . . . '

'Thanks, but it's not your apologies that I want. I want you to take a message to Cailean from me.'

'What message? I'll have no part in delivering threats or ultimatums.'

'Just tell him that I challenge him to an honourable duel. Tell him that I'll meet him at the foot of the Hermit's wood this afternoon. Tell him to bring a sword or a knife or something of that description along. Tell him that if he refuses, he will be looked upon as a coward.'

'Looked upon as a coward by whom?'

'Is he not a coward if he cannot accept the challenge of a man with one arm and one eye?'

Stephanos grimaced. 'I feel sorry for you, Cheiron Androcles. What do you define as cowardice? Could bravery spur a man on to killing another who is disabled?'

Cheiron looked at the minstrel framed in the doorway for a long time, his thoughts racing. He could not out talk a Bard. 'I am tired of your philosophy. Deliver my message.'

'And if I do not?'

'If you do not, I suggest that you tell your friend to be on his guard during the sleeping hours.'

Stephanos looked at him, disquieted, then he departed from the cave and Cheiron heard him bidding the Hermits farewell and rustling away through the long grass and cold air.

Cheiron was alone again, but for the Hermits sprawled on their rugs and snoring. Some time later, he got up and went out into the wood. He walked through the trees, stumbling up and down the hillside and pondering his current situation. He felt as though he was trapped in the Hermit's Wood for good. He stood above a sheer sandstone outcropping and looked through the trees, out on to the lands of the Brotherhood. There were people out there already, but he guessed that Kristabel was working somewhere else than on the lands adjacent to the Hermit's Wood because she was nowhere to be seen.

Disappointed at not seeing Kristabel, Cheiron walked slowly through the dew-wet grass, back to the encampment of the outlaws. There he remained all morning, squatting in the stinking, damp cave in which he had spent the night. He felt terrible after the night. He was unwashed, had spent the night sleeping on the damp floor of the cave whilst being fully dressed at the time. His body stank, the wounds to his face, hand and arm ached.

In the afternoon, he slipped away quietly and waited just inside the wood near the track that ran along the bottom of it. He waited impatiently for Cailean to arrive for a long time. He leant against a tree and looked out at the lands, glancing on occasion towards the Great House. He contemplated the architecture of the place, the stained glass window, the arches and the columns. He wondered by what method the people who had erected the Great House had hewn the sandstone blocks out of the rock. And still he waited. Then, in the middle of the afternoon, he saw a solitary figure walking along the track, coming from the direction of the village. He recognised the long, brown hair streaming from beneath the peculiar wide-brimmed hat. It was Cailean. Cheiron drew his sword from his belt where he had thrust it and held it awkwardly in his left hand. He stepped out on to the track and faced the man who was walking towards him.

Cailean stopped a few yards short of Cheiron and stared at him. 'I want no trouble with you, Cheiron Androcles . . . ' he began.

'You should have thought of that instead of becoming jealous for no reason and crying to the Brotherhood to do your dirty work for you.'

Cailean looked in a strange sort of awe at the mysterious figure with the single, shifting eye and the long, leather gauntlet hanging limp at his side beneath his cloak. 'You are evil. You are a demon. Do you think that I should let Kristabel fall into your hands?'

'You don't believe those stories any more than I do. You're just jealous of *me*. You think that I'm going to run off with your woman.'

'No! Demon!'

'I will argue with you no longer. Draw your blade and let this duel commence.'

Cailean drew a slender sword and a knife from two scabbards on his belt and took up the correct stance.

Cheiron described steady circles in the air with his sword and moved in close to his opponent. They circled each other slowly once or twice, and then Cheiron managed to entice Cailean to thrust with the short knife in his left hand. Cheiron swept the blow aside with his sword, and Cailean was forced to stoop down and to the left to avoid the long thrust that followed. He quickly jumped up from that position and grappled with Cheiron's sword arm from behind. Cheiron ducked and forced his sword into the ground, and with the same movement swung Cailean over his shoulder and on to the grass. Cheiron pulled out the sword and raised it to bring it down on to Cailean's head, but the tall man rolled out of the way and somersaulted to his feet again. He ran back at Cheiron, his face contorted with anger, and thrust quick jabs at Cheiron's ribs. Cheiron turned his body and took the thrust on the gauntlet which covered his useless right arm and hand. The sword cut into the gauntlet, and then Cailean overbalanced and fell at Cheiron's side. Cheiron turned to line up the death-blow with his left arm, and then he heard a familiar voice calling to him.

'Cheiron! No!' Kristabel shouted, picking up her skirts and running up the hill towards them.

Cheiron hesitated, then brought the sword down, but he only succeeded in smiting the mud of the track as Cailean sprang out of the way and seized him by the legs. Before he could do much about it, Cheiron felt himself falling. The two men, grappling awkwardly with their weapons went rolling down the hill. In the flurry of blows, both forgot about Kristabel, then some strange odour touched their noses and they looked up to see a thick, grey mist billowing over the fields. Cheiron kicked Cailean with all the force he could muster, and staggered up. Cailean fell back flailing and his head struck a stone lying in the grass. Cheiron adjusted his grip on the hilt of the sword, and moved to finish off the unconscious man, then remembered Kristabel. He turned to look for her, but she was obscured by the thickening mist. The terrible thought struck him: the mist of Izembard!

He ran down the hill and entered the cloud. He could see people fleeing from the dreaded fog, but some of the young girls remained, standing motionless. He heard the serene voice in the mist, the voice that sounded like perfection itself, the perfect female voice: 'THE PUREST NEED NOT FLEE. STAY, WELCOME MY SERVANTS. LET THEM BRING YOU TO ME. YOU ARE THE PURE IN HEART, THE CLEANEST OF YOUR SEX. YOU NEED NOT RUN FROM ME . . .'

At last, Cheiron spotted Kristabel, standing still in the mist, looking into the swirling, evil-smelling fog. Everywhere else now could only be seen as dark or light grey, the mist covered all. Then, in parts it began to darken into spinning columns of mist. These began to take on a form, and faint outlines of men began to appear. Slowly, the mist gathered around these until the creatures became solid and took on definite shape and colour. They were large brutes, with orange-brown skin which looked to be tough like old leather, and encrusted with filth and grime. They wore shiny black, segmented armour about their abdomens and carried heavy, cumbersome weapons in both hands. They had domed foreheads, overhanging small eyes set back into their heads. Their jaws were thrust forward and their mouths resembled those of apes. They had long, matted black hair which hung from a high hairline and trailed down their backs. They had large feet encased in heavy, thick-soled boots.

Cheiron moved into the mist, out of the sight of the Izembard creatures and tried to get close to Kristabel. The voice was omnipresent, in his ears and his mind. The rhythm of the voice was hypnotic, and he realised what effect it must have had on those to whom it was speaking: 'DO NOT FLEE, MY VIRGINAL LITTLE ONES. COME TO ME. LET MY SERVANTS BRING YOU TO ME . . .'

Cheiron glanced from side to side and saw that the creatures were appearing everywhere. The Hermits were defending their woodland home with swords and arrows, and the creatures of

Izembard defended themselves with their heat-rays, using them sparingly as it was clear that Kristabel had spoken the truth about them only having a single shot.

Cheiron looked back towards Kristabel, and saw that three of the creatures were advancing nervously towards her static form, panning their weapons to and fro.

'YOU HAVE NO NEED TO FLEE FROM ME, OH PUREST MAIDENS. STAY WHERE YOU ARE. MY SERVANTS WILL BRING YOU TO ME . . .'

Cheiron stayed in the cover of the mist and hoped that they would not see him. He became accustomed to the sound of the voice, and became aware of the sounds of the Hermits shouting and the occasional blast of the heat-rays. He wondered where the Brotherhood were, but then he realised that they were probably defending the people of the village from the creatures.

The three creatures were now very close to Kristabel. They approached her cautiously then one of them saw Cheiron's dark form in the mist. He levelled his heat-ray and Cheiron came running towards it. There was a very bright light, and a flurry of hissing sparks. Cheiron jumped to the ground and felt the heat of the ray pass over him. He jumped to his feet and ran forwards again, raising his sword. The other two turned to face him and fired their weapons simultaneously. Both missed, Cheiron running between the rays. Then he was upon them, and the blade hacked into their leathery flesh. They wrestled with him, but two of them fled when their companion sank to the grass with a sword through his throat. The life gone from the fallen wretch, his body offered no resistance to the harmful chemicals which encrusted his skin, and he disintegrated in seconds. Cheiron seized Kristabel's arm and tried to shake her out of the trance, but the voice was stronger: 'COME, COME TO ME. BE NOT AFRAID, PURE IN HEART. YOU ARE THE CLEANEST OF YOUR SEX. COME TO ME . . .'

Another group of the creatures came out of the mist towards Cheiron and Kristabel. Cheiron motioned forwards, then felt the pain between his shoulder blades, and he knew as soon as he felt the sharp and sudden agony that it was a mortal wound. The blade had impaled his lungs. He felt his breath constrict, and blood welled up in his throat and seeped out of the corner of his mouth. A second later, three parallel heat-rays cut through the mist and Cailean screamed, and fell backwards with his clothing erupting into flame, and the blood dripping from the knife in his hand.

Kristabel saw Cheiron fall to the grass. He collapsed to his knees, looked up at her and then toppled to one side and was still. She looked down at him, and pain wracked her mind as the voice of the Countess of Izembard was driven from her mind by the shock of seeing the two men die before her eyes. Her forehead tingled as she felt the blotch of red stain her white skin. She fell to her knees at Cheiron's side, and the mist began to thin as the Brotherhood rode by on either side of them, their swords whirling in the air, chasing the fleeing creatures of Izembard.

Kristabel looked at Cheiron's face, his eyes were closed, and it was strange for her to think that he was not just sleeping. He was dead, unthinking, unheeding. A glistening thread of scarlet came from the side of his mouth. She glanced behind Cheiron and saw Cailean lying in the grass, small flames dancing on his body. His hair was burnt away, and his face charred and burnt beyond recognition. Kristabel felt a tear run down her cheek. Cailean was dead, Cheiron Androcles . . . was dead.

Epilogue

They stood at the graveside, Calisto in her light dress and shawl, with the cool wind reddening her cheeks and blowing her hair, and Kristabel in her heavy cloak, her greying, wispy hair streaming.

Calisto read the inscription on the ornate marker:

'BEHOLD THE LOVE WARRIOR,
MIGHTY IN THE HEART,
BUT WEAKENED IN THE SOUL.
BEHOLD THE BLADE,
THE BLADE THAT THIRSTS
FOR A BLEEDING HEART,
TO REPAY THE LOSS OF THE SLAYER.'

'I have been here many times, and each time I think that this inscription says very little that is good about my father.'

'Try not to confuse love and goodness, Calisto. Cheiron would have approved of the inscription; he loved the truth as well as other, more tangible things.'

'Did you grieve him greatly, Kristabel?'

'Him, and Cailean. I loved them both. How can a woman love two men? Perhaps neither of them would have died if I had not . . .'

Calisto touched Kristabel's arm. 'Don't blame yourself, Kristabel, please.'

Kristabel sighed. 'It was a long time ago, I do not grieve so much now. The virgin-blotch which the creatures from Izembard put on my forehead is gone. What, then, of your life?'

'I wish to do what my father set out to do.'

'To follow his quest?'

Calisto nodded slowly. 'To its end.'

Kristabel put her hand inside her cloak and unfastened a chain around her neck. She brought out a pendant, heavy and circular, and pressed it into Calisto's hand. 'Take this. It was Cheiron's. It was given to Cailean as a reward for telling the Brotherhood about Cheiron and me going to Stoney Clouds. The Brotherhood took it from him when they tortured him. They knew not what it was.'

Calisto examined it. 'It is the sign of Lord Satan, like the one you said my father told you he had taken from the man who tried to kill him on another world.'

'It is the one. Keep it. You will notice it also bears representations of the other Lords besides the Devil.'

'Thank you, Kristabel.'

'Now, you must leave.'

'Leave? Where? How?'

'I hear that there are Tellers in the Hermit's Wood of late. They will take you. You have nothing here but memories. Your father and mother are dead, I will soon be an old woman. Go to the Hermit's Wood.'

Calisto knelt beside the gravestone and ran her fingers over its rough surface. *Can I leave her? It is so sudden, just to walk away from my home. What would my Father have had me do?* She turned to speak to Kristabel, but she was gone. She walked away up the road to the farm, and Calisto was alone. She turned back to the stone: 'BEHOLD THE LOVE WARRIOR . . . ' She stood up and looked to the Hermit's Wood. She pulled her shawl tighter about her shoulders, and after a moment's meditation, she departed from the graveside, leaving a silent prayer of farewell.